Freakn'
Cougar

(Freakn' Shifters, Book Six)

Eve Langlais

Copyright © January 2014, Eve Langlais
Cover Art by Amanda Kelsey © December 2013
Edited by Devin Govaere
Copy Edited by Amanda L. Pederick
Produced in Canada

Published by Eve Langlais
1606 Main Street, PO Box 151
Stittsville, Ontario, Canada, K2S1A3
http://www.EveLanglais.com

ISBN-13: 978 1988 328 24 9

Chapter One

Sunday was family dinner night. For most people this would mean a loving gathering of close relatives around the supper table, exchanging news and exciting gossip over home-cooked food.

But his was no ordinary family. With the exception of one new addition, all present were shapeshifters; large cats, wolves, and even one big-ass bear. As for Stu, one of the lupine diners, he was related, in an unfortunate twist of fate, to all of them.

To one side of him sat Chris, younger brother, pain in his ass, and newly married chump to the lovely and delicate Jiao. On his right, he had the entertaining Alejandro, his other brother Mitchell—whom he lived to tease—and feisty Francine, their mate as well as his sister's best friend.

Across the table sat his loud-mouthed, bratty sister Naomi with her mates Ethan and Javier, accompanied by his adorable baby niece and nephew—who currently took turns spitting out food and chortling. Then there was his other brother Kendrick, his best bud Joel, and their human mate, Ruth, a plump and juicy morsel. Not that he said that aloud—he preferred to not bleed all over his favorite *Despicable Me* minion T-shirt.

His oldest brother, Derrick, was the only one of his siblings missing because he was off on some mission to save the world—he always had been an overachiever and champion ass-kisser.

Toss in his mom and dad at the heads of the

table, and the noise level currently underway probably exceeded local bylaw levels. Not that anyone would dare complain. Their neighbors were shapeshifters too and would more likely pee on the leg of a ticketing bylaw agent than complain about one of their own.

Seeing as how the whole family was pretty much accounted for, it made the ringing of the doorbell surprising. What insane person would show up at dinnertime on a Sunday at his house? Then again, the table still had one empty seat, a seat his mother enjoyed glancing toward at least once a day before shooting him a pointed stare, a look that plainly said, "And when will you be settling down with a mate of your own?"

As if he'd be filling it anytime soon. He still intended to sow many more oats before settling down. Of course, the whole sowing thing required him leaving the house and going to places where he could meet girls. Stu wasn't the social type. At least not in person.

While comfortable around close friends and family, Stu lacked a suave tongue when it came to conversing with women. Tongue-tied, shy, and awkward tended to strike whenever he tried to flirt. So he mostly stuck to online dating personals, which would work a lot better if most of the profiles didn't belong to lonely old men getting their jollies. Stu still woke in a cold sweat every so often when he remembered the video of the last so-called woman he'd virtually dated. Needless to say, *she* turned out to be a very hairy *he* who enjoyed masturbating for an audience while wearing a bunny rabbit suit. It took a week for the blindness to wear off.

Before the chimes could ding a second time, his father excused himself to answer, not that anyone paid much attention. The various conversation threads flowed fast and furious as everyone caught up on the week's events. Naomi and Francine gushed over the newest thing the wonder twins had accomplished while the guys all discussed the most recent roster changes on the Ottawa Senators line-up.

Stu paid little of it any mind. He just came down from his room to scarf down a plateful, inhale some of mom's pie, and store some energy for the World of Warcraft attack he'd planned with a group of other online gamers for the evening. His level seventy-six mage had acquired some new spells and armor that he was dying to test out.

But, judging by his stirring wolf, those plans might get cancelled.

Something smelled good, and for once it wasn't Ma's homemade peach cobbler pie. Leaning back in his seat and ignoring the noise around him, Stu inhaled deep, sifting the various scents.

No doubt about it. A shifter had entered their home. Someone he'd never met, in person at least. A female. *Sniff. Sniff.* Feline. And coming this way.

Stu opened his eyes and saw her as she stepped into the dining room, a trim, thirty-something blonde with bobbed hair and vivid blue eyes. Damn, talk about hot! She looked like a man's stripper fantasy in her perfectly pressed RCMP uniform, which, while stern, did nothing to hide her athletic build, softened by very womanly curves. But it wasn't just her looks that caught his attention, more the fact that judging by the way his inner beast sat up and took notice, along with a certain body part, he'd just found his mate.

What an unexpected surprise. Not that she was older than him or a cat, but the fact he even had a mate. Still in his twenties—and, yes, twenty-nine counted—his track record with women wasn't great. While at ease among friends and family, he turned into a bumbling idiot around women he found appealing. Even when he did manage to speak, his appearance often played against him.

Stu was into comfort. Well-worn jeans, T-shirts with cartoons and humorous sayings, oh and hair he let his mother trim, usually while licking the mixing bowl for the brownies, her bribe to get him to sit still while she hacked at his uneven locks.

Don't get him wrong. While he wasn't movie star handsome, he also wasn't butt ugly. Just ask his momma.

Sitting ramrod straight in his seat, he plastered a smile on his face, wished he'd combed his hair, and hoped nothing was stuck between his teeth. Alas, despite his certainty that the woman who'd entered was his mate, his luck with women held true. Her eyes tracked over him and didn't linger. So much for instant attraction. On the upside, at least she didn't scream, gag, or run away.

"Patricia, grab a seat," his mom yelled from the kitchen, not at all perturbed by the addition of another person at their rollicking, mismatched dining table.

His mind automatically began to hum *Patricia Delicia*. Great stripper song, but not the time for it.

He shoved aside the naughty ditty sung by that crooner Chris De Burgh as he tried to concentrate on placing the woman. Why did her name sound so familiar? Surely if they'd met before he would remember.

With a husky voice that would have done well on a late-night radio show, she replied, "I can't. I'm here on business. I'm looking for Stu Grayson."

Business involving him? Given her attire and the seriousness of her tone, that couldn't bode well. Had his illegal pirating of movies and MP3s finally caught up to him because, as far as he knew, surfing porn—and whacking off to it—wasn't illegal. What were the chances he could slink off his chair, hide under the table, and sneak out the back door? Given the fact a Chihuahua wouldn't make it through the maze of legs and feet, not good.

Only one thing to do. Man up and hope for the best.

Stu pushed back from the table, his chair screeching on the battered hardwood floor, and stood. "That's me. What can I do for you?"

"Stu Grayson, I'm placing you under arrest." Patricia dangled a set of metal cuffs, and jaws all over the place dropped. Except for Chris'. He laughed his face off as he shouted, "About time you came for him. Remember not to bend over in the slammer, big bro."

Mitchell, not one to pass up an opportunity, muttered to Alejandro, "Guess my geeky brother finally hacked the wrong site. At least now I know what to get him for Christmas. Lube!" They both guffawed.

Jerks. He'd get them back later. Digital manipulation was a wonderful weapon. Right now, though, Stu had an important matter requiring his attention; how to impress the sexy cougar.

Being somewhat of a smartass, when bolstered by an audience that had his back, Stu couldn't help but reply, "Honey, if you've got handcuffs, I'll go with you anywhere." The guys at the table snickered. The women didn't. Especially the woman in question.

A pursing of her lips was all the reaction he got, not even a blush. Then, again, in her line of work, she probably dealt with stupid come-on lines all the time. *Mate or not, I don't think I'm making a great first impression.*

Thankfully, he had his family around him, ready to make the situation worse.

"Exactly what do you want my brother for?" Naomi demanded, standing up from her seat, her babies handed off to her mates as she glared at the cougar who didn't cower.

Brave girl. Not many in his family liked to get in his baby sister's way when she got her hackles up. Naomi could throw an evil left hook. And she fought dirty. His testicles still shriveled into pathetic grapes when she turned her ire his way.

Before Naomi could do any damage, Chris hopped to his feet. "Before you tackle her to the ground and entertain us all with a girl fight, why don't we let Patricia explain? I'm sure she has a good explanation for why Stu here needs to visit the big house."

Patricia. Why oh why did that name sound so

familiar? He snapped his fingers. "I know who you are. You're that RCMP broad who was helping Jiao and her brother out." While he knew of her, they'd never actually crossed paths, but he'd heard enough of her via Chris and his mate to know she was supposed to be good people. No one had told him, though, what a hottie she was.

"Correct, and would you mind not referring to me as *that broad*?"

Icy blue eyes met his, and was it stupid of him to feel a touch of disappointment that they didn't regard him with any kind of warmth or interest? His wolf whined in his head. Was he mistaken about the mating bond? Could he just be suffering from good ol' fashioned lust?

"Sorry, honey." He tried to adopt an apologetic mien but failed miserably judging by his brother's snicker.

"That's it, bro, keep shoving your foot in your mouth," Mitchell said in a low breath.

"How about we stick to ma'am."

Mmm, take-charge kind of woman. He could handle that. A broad grin stretched his lips. "Yes, ma'am."

Perhaps that came out a little more fervently than it should have, or worshipful, still though, it didn't merit her forbearing sigh and slight shake of her head. And did he hear a muttered, "Pup," spoken in a derisive tone?

Pup? Why, he was in his late twenties, practically middle-aged. So what if he still lived at home and had both an Xbox and a PlayStation in his room? Plenty of grown men did nowadays. Nothing wrong with being young at heart.

His dad offered Patricia the empty seat while his mom served her up a plate of pie.

She tried to wave it away. "I really can't stay. I'm here on official business."

"You can explain it over a cup of coffee and dessert," his mother said, pushing Patricia into the chair. Patricia wisely didn't fight, else it might have gotten interesting. His mother expected people to obey her edicts and wasn't above force-feeding a guest if she thought they needed some more meat on their bones.

"I guess I can spare a minute. It's the least I can do given I'm about to arrest your son."

"What did he do this time?" His dad didn't even give him the benefit of the doubt.

"Hey, I resent that," Stu protested. "It's not my fault I've gotten in trouble a couple of times with the law." Misunderstandings in his mind for the most part. How was he supposed to know that the fact he could easily hack his high school's website and post an image of the principal making out with the kindergarten teacher was wrong? They were doing it on school property. Didn't that make it school news? And as for the time he'd gotten arrested for indecent exposure for peeing in the alley? He wasn't alone in using that spot as a public urinal. He'd just been the slowest to zip and too drunk to run without bouncing off a brick wall right into the arresting officer's arms.

"What are the charges?" his dad asked.

In the midst of taking a bite of Mom's famous apple pie, Patricia took her time answering. "I can't really say."

"What? Why not?" Naomi posed the query everyone was surely thinking.

"I'm with her, and not just because we're married. Since when do you arrest someone and not give a reason?" Ethan asked in a rumble that cut through the noise.

"Would you accept the fact this is classified shifter business and leave it at that?"

The emphatic "No" followed by laughter answered that.

Patricia squirmed in her seat, glanced around the table, and sighed. "I told my bosses you'd have questions. Listen, what I say can't leave this room. Can I count on you all to keep quiet?"

Curious glances abounded, but one by one, his family nodded, and Stu found himself more interested than ever in what the hot cougar had to say, and not just because he enjoyed her gravelly voice. He smelled a mystery.

"As far as the outside world is concerned, I'm arresting Stu. I'm not one hundred percent sure on what grounds, other than the fact it's going to involve him pleading guilty and getting sent to a federal penitentiary."

No one could stop the tsunami of questions that statement caused. Stu didn't add to the cacophony, but he did catch the blonde's eye and raise a single brow in query. This time she held his gaze, her brow wrinkling slightly as if puzzled.

It was his mother with a quietly, but firmly, spoken, "Explain," that killed the hubbub and broke their staring match.

"It's complicated and supposed to be hush hush."

Jiao placed her hand atop Patricia's. "You can trust them to keep a secret."

"I hope so because the last thing we need is for this to get out and send the person we're really hunting underground."

"Sounds serious."

"It is. We have a series of crimes that have been happening all across Canada in federal jails."

"And this concerns us how?" His dad leaned forward in his seat, pie forgotten, as he waited for an answer.

"Shifters are being killed."

"Prisoners?"

"Yes."

"In jail?"

"Yes."

"So why do we care that sentenced criminals are getting offed, and what does this have to do with Stu?" Mitchell asked what most of them were thinking. In their world, they tended to view things rather black and white, and not just because of their wolf genes. If you did the crime, you did the time.

Back in the old days, before the laws and civilization became mainstream, shifter packs used to live by the motto of an eye for an eye. Literally. Killers were executed. Thieves lost everything, including their thieving hands. Rapists ... well, let's just say they never committed the same crime twice.

If shifters were in jail, especially federal jail, then it was because they'd done something serious. If they were getting killed, it was probably tragic to their families, but a blessing to the victims they'd left behind. It still didn't explain why Patricia had business with him. Stu certainly hadn't done anything that merited federal jail time and he certainly had nothing to do with shifters getting killed. The only killing he did was virtually, usually with a kick ass spell.

"We all should care, despite the fact they're outlaws, because whoever is doing it is making it look like accidents, or suicide. And they're only targeting shifters, no matter what they're doing time for. The last one killed was only in there for tax evasion. The one before for owning a marijuana grow op. Actually, none of the shifters killed were in for anything violent. The shifter council prefers to take care of those cases themselves, as you well know."

Because a psycho killer or raping sentient animal was not just a menace to the public at large but a threat to them all. A shifter who lost respect for their laws and others often didn't care about exposure.

"Could it be a vigilante at work? Someone who is worried that the close quarters of prison will reveal our secret?"

"A theory we pondered, except, in some cases, the prisoners had been there more than ten years without anyone catching wind of their secret. No matter their reasoning, they don't have the right to kill."

"How come we haven't heard of this?" Stu's father broached.

"It only recently came to light. The deaths were spread out among various institutions and took place over the past two years. As well, most were classed as accidents or suicide. It wasn't until recently that we caught on to the pattern."

"How many have died?"

Patricia's lips flattened into a straight line. "More than thirty-seven by our count."

Chaos once again erupted as shouts of "How could no one notice?" and "Who's responsible?" fired at the cougar from all directions.

Stu ignored his mother's awesome pie to mull over the little they'd learned so far. The one thing Patricia had yet to explain was how he tied into the whole affair. Stu certainly wasn't the killer they were seeking. Nor was he a victim or related to one. As the yelling continued all around him, he mulled Patricia's presence until he had his "Aha!" moment.

"Am I getting paid for you to use me as bait?" His query arrowed through the din and resulted in utter silence, a few dropped jaws, and shocked, wide-open eyes.

Of course, the quiet didn't last more than two seconds before the noise got even worse than before with Naomi practically crawling over the table determined to rearrange Patricia's face and thinking. In Naomi's world, only she was allowed to abuse her brothers. It was nice to be loved.

But Naomi wasn't the only one weighing in on the situation. Chris shouted advice about not dropping the soap while his mother declared they'd use him over her dead body. As for his dad? From under bushy brows, he just glared all around.

Given the varying opinions and shouting, was it any wonder Stu found himself desperate to escape so he could think? On second thought, why couldn't he?

He slunk from the room and exited to his backyard. Hands in his pockets, he peered at the stars, which shone brightly in the clear night sky.

Despite Patricia not getting a true chance to answer him, dangling him as bait or using him to ferret out information from the inside were the only things that made sense. They needed Stu to catch a killer. Why or how they expected him to help, he couldn't have said. He possessed no training that would aid in an investigation, nothing legal at any rate. But, if they were looking for someone who knew how to hack a firewall or dig up information on a computer hard drive, intel thought deleted or buried, well, he wasn't known as the sneaky wolf in hacking circles for nothing.

But why the arresting ruse? Why not just come out and ask him?

His absence from the dinner table didn't go unnoticed; however, it wasn't his family who came looking for him. Her scent enveloped him, and awareness spiked through his frame, tingling along his nerve endings and making his heart race faster.

She's here. His wolf practically pranced in delight. Out here in the fresh air, he could inhale her sweet aroma and know without a doubt that, yes, she was meant for him. But how did one broach that topic with an almost virtual stranger? Somehow, saying, "Hey, honey, my wolf wants to take a bite," seemed a tad forward. He'd gotten enough slaps over the years to know most women did not appreciate the honest and direct approach. Unlike his brothers, he sucked at flirting. Was it any wonder he preferred to spend his time in front of a computer screen?

"I wondered if you'd run," she said, breaking the silence.

"I thought about it."

"Why didn't you?"

He shrugged. "I don't understand what you want me for, but that doesn't mean I'm going to take the cowardly route and bolt before I find out."

"You know enough by now that if you want me to walk away, I will. No one, not even the shifter council, can force you to lend a helping hand."

"Walk away?" He snorted. "Have you met my family? I'd never live it down. Beside, I'm curious."

"And yet you're not a cat." A dryly spoken jest that eased the tension somewhat.

Shyness wouldn't let him look directly at her. "I'm surprised my family let you slip away," he said. "I would have thought they'd duct tape you to a chair and interrogate you until Ma beat them off with a wooden spoon."

"Yeah, your sister did threaten to sit on me and tap my forehead with a finger until I confessed everything, but her mate, Ethan, carted her out of the room before she could tackle me. After that little tussle, I told them I needed to use the girl's room. Given how busy the rest of them were arguing with each other, I figure I have a few minutes before they notice I'm gone."

He angled his head slightly so he could see her face in profile. So pretty. So confident. So not the type who usually let him get near them. Fate sure had a sense of humor trying to set him up with someone so obviously out of his league.

"Was I right? Is that what you're here for? To dangle me as bait?"

"Yes, and no. Obviously, we don't want any civilians to get hurt, but it's possible, especially given we intend to place you in with the prisoners. So, yes, in one sense, you could be perceived as bait."

"Not exactly selling it," he jested.

"Just being honest. You should know what the mission entails."

"Why do I get the impression you're telling me more than I'm supposed to know?"

"Because I am. My orders were to march in here, arrest you, book you, and more or less railroad you into the system then fill you in on the plan."

"Why change it?"

"Because I've met most of your family. I like them. Respect them. They deserve better than the secrecy the shifter council seems to think is necessary."

"Not to mention, their plan would have seen my family raising a holy stink. At least now, if they think my arrest serves a higher purpose, they'll raise hell, as folks would expect, but not bust me out."

"They'd do that?"

Stu chuckled. "In a heartbeat. My mother might rule us with an iron paw and sturdy spoon, but no one hurts her babies."

"I'm glad I followed my gut then."

"So, I'm going to jail. Why me? Why not someone in the RCMP? Or someone working for the shifter council?"

"We've already maxed out those personnel

trying to cover all bases. We fell short. We still need someone with not just a tarnished record to make it believable but certain skills. Computer skills."

"You want me to hack the prison system? Why not just get me in under the guise of repairman then? Or as a data entry clerk? Why go through the motions of arresting me?"

"Because we're not sure whoever is doing this is part of the system. We need someone on the inside, undercover and part of the population. A technician or prison employee isn't going to hear or have access to the same information."

Disparaging or not, he had to say it. "You do realize I don't really look the part of bad-ass criminal." While a big guy with his fair share of muscles, Stu was more like the Shaggys of the world. Long-haired, easygoing, hippy dude, not tattooed, scary-looking biker.

"Trust me. I noticed." She had? Now why did she make such a moue when she said it? "Which is why you won't be alone in there."

"I'm getting a jailhouse partner?"

"Yes. He is everything you're not. Or so my contact on the shifter council claims."

"You haven't met him?"

A shake of her head sent her blonde bob swinging. "No. He's already in place, gathering information."

"And what's your part in this, honey?"

"I thought we'd discussed you not calling me that."

His lips quirked. "You demanded. But, given I'm about to become a criminal, I think it's time I learned how to diss the law."

"Diss?" She snorted. "Yeah, more and more, I'm beginning to think you're the wrong guy for the job."

What?

Before he could ask her why, she spun on her heel and walked away. It took him only a few strides to catch her. He gripped her arm to halt her.

Awareness slammed into him. Shocked blue eyes met his, and they engaged in a staring match. He leaned in. She didn't move away. He shuffled closer. Her lips parted.

"Stu! Get your hairy ass back in here and bring the kitty too!" Naomi shouted.

The moment shattered.

Stu sighed as Patricia moved away. "You really should have stuck to just arresting me and saying nothing. In case you hadn't noticed, my family tends to get involved in each other's business."

"Trust me. I'm kicking myself," she muttered.

She might already regret her actions, but he didn't. On the contrary, Stu found himself the most excited he ever recalled. Even more so than when he'd spent thirty-six hours outside Best Buy waiting for the release of the newest Black Ops game.

Forget a gaming mission. He was about to *live* a mission. Be the hero. And, if lucky, get the girl.

"Stu! Don't make me drag you in by your long hair," Naomi screeched.

He sighed. *Yeah, I'll be a hero and get my cougar only if I can get away from my family.*

Chapter Two

It took another hour of explaining, more pie, a few cookies, and promises to keep them in the loop before Stu's family let her leave with him. He, on the other hand, didn't say much. He just sat back and watched Patricia. It should have creeped her out. Instead, Patricia found herself all too aware of him, and she didn't like it one bit. Only once before had she felt that level of awareness, that electric shock of recognition. That hadn't turned out well for her in the end. So this time, despite the urging of her cougar, she ignored it.

Not an easy task. Once she got Stu alone, she'd hoped to regain her equilibrium, but failed. Heck, she had to fight the urge to roll down all the windows and stick her head out the open space to suck in fresh air. It wasn't that the guy in the backseat of her cruiser stank. On the contrary, Stu smelled good. *Really* good. Tempting. He also smelled like trouble. *Because if my nose is not mistaken and my cougar can be believed, then he's my freakn' mate.*

Which was impossible. *I have a mate.* Make that had one. She'd buried him years ago after a motorcycle accident. She'd loved and lost and mourned Ryker. She'd gotten on with life, more or less, like any shifter did who lost the other half of their soul. She'd resigned herself to a future of dating and being the spinster at functions because everyone knew shifters only got one mate.

One.

No second chances.

So what did her racing heart, boiling blood, nose twitching, nipple tingling sensations for a guy young enough for her to have babysat while he was still in diapers mean? Okay, maybe not that much younger than her, probably only about ten years, but still. *He is not my mate.*

Explain that, though, to her pacing cat, who prowled her mind insisting otherwise.

Tell that to the teasing scent of him that enveloped her and taunted her senses.

Point that out to her body, which roused with erotic interest, insidiously whispering to her that she should pull over and run her fingers through his hair, rub her lips along his, and ride him to a screaming climax the likes she'd not experienced since Ryker.

She gritted her teeth and kept her focus on the road and the task at hand. Get him to RCMP headquarters to book him. Then go home for a long, icy-cold shower.

"Run the plan by me again," Stu asked from the backseat, the partition between them not enough to block his disturbing presence. "Maybe, this time, I can grasp all the finer details without my family adding its two cents and threats of violence every other sentence."

"Speaking of which, what's up with your brother Chris and his shower references? He does realize that kind of thing doesn't usually happen, right?"

"Blame television," Stu replied with a grin she caught in her rear-view mirror.

"It almost sounds like he wants you to get

hurt."

"Hurt? No. Embarrassed? Most definitely."

"Your family is … different."

His laughter washed over her in a warm wave. "How diplomatic. You can say it like it is, you know. They're freakn' nuts. Violent nuts. But I love 'em anyway."

Having no clear recollection of her parents, Patricia couldn't quite understand how one could survive in such a dysfunctional group and emerge sane, but having met most of the Graysons as a result of her relationship with Jiao, Chris' mate, she wouldn't deny the family was tight knit. And crazy. Most definitely crazy.

She returned their conversation to the task she'd originally set out to complete before getting side-tracked. "As I mentioned before, we've linked a series of shifter deaths in prisons."

"No humans, eh?"

"It's possible a few might have gotten killed. However, for simplicity, we've stuck to investigating only the shifter ones."

"I take it they weren't doing time for the same types of crime."

"Nope. Their reasons for being there ranged from tax fraud to drugs to major theft. Nothing to link them. The ages of the victims range from early twenties to late thirties."

"No old fogeys? Or are there not any old men in jail?"

"There are some, but we've ruled out the deaths of those as actual natural causes."

"So explain to me again why the council

thinks these deaths are murders. You said something about them being classed as accidents or suicides. Why the change of heart?"

"Because, on the surface, that's how they appeared. But a few of the ones deemed suicide caused a stink with the families. They insisted their loved one would never take their own life. We began to take a closer look and found some disturbing patterns. For one, many of them had details fudged over in the reports."

"How did you figure that out?"

"First-hand accounts of people who populated the cells around the victims and autopsy reports. Some of the families had drug panels done. They came up positive for a tranquilizing agent usually mixed with something else."

Stu didn't ask stupid questions such as how could inmates get drugs in prison. No matter how many protocols they put into place, the black-market thrived in the penitentiaries. Despite screening, drugs got into prisons. Loved ones brought them, prisoners found ways to have them smuggled in, guards could be bribed or were corrupt to start with. Where money was involved, illegal trade existed.

"Were they known drug users?" he queried.

She shook her head. "In most of the cases, it was a definite no. And, in all the cases, the drug that was found in their blood work was nowhere to be found in their cell."

"It could have been stolen or moved."

"Possibly. But the drug in question isn't exactly high on the list of wanted substances."

"I'm guessing it wasn't some munchyinducing Mary Jane but something a little more obscure then?"

"Try Rohypnol."

His reflection in the mirror showed his brows rising. "The date rape drug?"

"The one and only, which is the first oddity. As you can imagine, Rohypnol is not high on the list of smuggled contraband. Ecstasy, marijuana, and cocaine, yes, but a drug to drop someone into a comatose like state? Not so much."

"That doesn't make sense. Someone slips the guys a mickey in order to take advantage of them? How does that work?" Stu couldn't hide the questioning note. "I mean guys need to *feel* to be able to perform or at least get a boner. Were they given Viagra too?"

"No."

That left only one thing a sexual predator could do to a male. His butt clenched tight. "Did they at least use lube?"

"No. Despite the drug used, this isn't a crime about sex. Which is what makes it so odd. I mean there are much better drugs out there to use to incapacitate a shifter. Like ketamine. Why use Rohypnol?"

"So after the guy is taken down, what happens next?"

"This is where it differs a little. We've come across three scenarios that seem to repeat with no specific pattern. In one, the shifter seems to commit suicide."

"How can you *seem* to?"

"Because how many shifters do you know

that would use a blade to cut their own wrists to bleed out?" Not to mention, most shifters didn't usually kill themselves. Most who opted to end their lives did so in a violent fashion by going wild, literally, and finding the biggest predator around and engaging in a battle to the death. Their death. Of course, a prison would restrict them somewhat, but given the badasses populating them, easy enough to accomplish.

"The guys slit their wrists with, let me guess, a blade that can't be found?"

"You got it."

"Why use a blade when we have teeth?"

"Another sticky point."

"Didn't the people investigating wonder why they couldn't find the weapon?"

"Weapons never stick around in prison. Everyone always assumes someone else scooped it."

"What's the second scenario?"

"Garrotte."

"As in choke themselves to death with what? A sock?"

She hesitated saying it aloud because even to her, who'd read the reports, it sounded ridiculous. But Stu was waiting. "Underpants."

To his credit, he didn't outright laugh, but he sound incredulous when he said, "Seriously?"

She bobbed her head.

"Unfreakn' believable." He couldn't help his sarcasm from showing through when he added, "Let me guess, those are usually missing too?"

"No. But they don't belong to the prisoner either."

"Geez, this is getting weird."

"No, this is weird. The third accidental deaths are drowning."

"How does someone drown in a cell?" He no sooner asked than he uttered, "Oh. *Ooooh.*" He blew out a breath. "The ultimate swirly. What a rotten way to go."

"No kidding. But, again, not totally unheard of if someone is desperate enough to die. Thing is, none of these shifters showed signs of depression, no warning signs at all."

"Not to mention the drug in their system would have rendered them virtually comatose. So the question is, how did they manage to do it?" Stu sat back in the seat, and his face took on a pensive expression as he mulled the information.

She continued to talk. "The prison officials took the easy route of declaring them suicides, but once we began to notice a pattern emerging, especially the shifter link, and once the evidence of Rohypnol was discovered, the shifter council put together a task force."

"According to what you said before, I'm not the only one going undercover. There are others."

"The pattern seems to be the perp infiltrates the prison, kills off all the shifters serving time, then moves on to the next prison. Since each prison has, so far, only been hit once, they've assigned six officers in provinces across Canada to go undercover in the federal pens that have so far remained untouched."

"Who's organizing this investigation? The shifters council or the RCMP? Because I thought you said the humans didn't suspect a thing."

"They don't. But the council pulled a few strings, and I'm going undercover for the RCMP under the guise of looking for drugs. It's also how we're getting you in there."

"So we're going on a fake mission, undercover, to uncover a real crime."

"Um, exactly. I think."

He grinned. "Cool. So what's your secret identity? My hot girlfriend who visits me? We can exchange secrets in the conjugal trailer. Or will you be the warden who calls me in for personal one-on-one punishment?"

"Dream on, wolfboy. My role will be that of prison guard. Bitchy prison guard," she added with a smirk.

"That doesn't sound too safe. Federal pens are where the worst of the worst go."

Just like a man to doubt her skills and training. "I can take care of myself. I have a baton, and I know how to use it."

"I'm sure you do."

The innuendo wasn't lost on her, and for a moment, their eyes met in the mirror, and a bolt of pure lust hit her, right between the legs. Her body temperature rose, moisture pooled, her womb clenched—

She tore her gaze away and focused on the road. "We've got someone reworking the prison guard schedule. I'll be transferring in under an alias a day or so after your arrival."

"You mean you're throwing me to the lions alone."

"Not entirely. I did mention you'd have a roommate."

"Another cop?"

"Oh no. This guy's a criminal. Badass through and through, or so I've heard."

"How reassuring."

"Actually, I should have phrased that as, he was a badass. He's reformed now supposedly. Saw the light and all that. Currently he works helping juveniles to get out of gangs and off the streets."

"Sounds like a saint. He a hacker too?"

"No. Think of him as muscle. Part of his job, other than making friends with the more unsavory elements, is to keep your lily-white ass safe from those who might be tempted to see what it looks like when you do bend over to grab that bar of soap."

"Oh, no, please don't tell me he's going to be my—"

She laughed. "Ricky, short for Ricardo, is your new cell-mate boyfriend."

"I am never going to live this down," Stu muttered.

They talked the remaining few minutes of the ride, just more of the basics on what she knew and what they wanted him to do. Basically, dig around and see what he could find without getting caught.

In no time at all, she had him booked and jailed. As another officer led him away, she couldn't help but watch and thus caught the panicked look tossed over his shoulder. Despite his bravado in the backseat of her cruiser, he obviously had his doubts.

She almost called the whole thing off then and there. How could she let him walk into danger?

He was a civilian. An innocent. She should be protecting him from criminals, not thrusting him among them. She bit her tongue and turned away.

Since when did she give a damn? Stu was no different than any other person conscripted to help on a tough case. Then why could she not stop thinking of him alone in his cell? *You know why,* her cat seemed to say, circling in her mind, agitated in a way she'd not seen in years.

While Stu got introduced to his new home, she tried to wrap her mind around the fact that her body and cougar seemed convinced he was her mate.

No way.

Sure, she found him cute, and even if he was younger than her, attractive and eminently doable, but no way would she open herself up to the kind of pain she'd gone through when Ryker died. Losing her mate, the love of her life, had hurt. It hurt so freakn' bad. She'd thought she'd die of the loneliness and heartache. She'd vowed to never let another man, anyone really for that matter, get that close to her again. Why bother caring? In the end, it would only lead to pain. It was why she kept herself aloof, removed from everyone. Never let anyone get too close. The only exception was Jiao and her brother. Their plight and horrifying story touched her. She couldn't help but come to their rescue and keep them out of harm's way, recognizing kindred spirits who'd borne too much trauma in their young lives already. Everyone else though? They only ever scratched the surface.

It wasn't the most perfect of plans, but it worked. It kept her going when she wanted to give up. It kept her sane when the loneliness became too much. It sucked, but the alternative in her mind was worse. *Caring for someone means hurting if you lose them.* No thank you. Been there. Done that. And she had no desire to repeat the experience.

How dare fate intervene just when she'd constructed an impermeable wall around her heart? How dare fate mess with her perfectly good life plan? Throwing a man her way indeed. Trying to tempt her into feeling again. Not happening. She'd just have to fight the urge. Heck, for all she knew, she just suffered from some about-to-turn-forty jitters, a subconscious panic that made her think Stu was her mate in an attempt to keep her young when, in fact, all she needed was some good raunchy, no-strings, emotionless sex.

Now if only Stu were here instead of languishing in a cell so she could cure herself of her problem.

Chapter Three

Twenty-eight. Twenty-nine. Ricky counted the push-ups in his head, the steady cadence of exercise soothing and calming to his churning mind.

Undercover almost a month and Ricky had yet to uncover a single clue or even a rumor about a killer targeting shifters. *Don't tell me I got assigned to the wrong prison.* An anger he'd fought long and hard to master threatened to bubble up.

When the shifter council approached him after the death of his brother—*say it like it is, his murder*—he'd jumped on the chance to help them mete out justice. He'd known the suicide verdict couldn't be true. His little brother Joey would never have killed himself, and certainly not by slitting his wrists.

Shapeshifter or not, Joey hated the sight of blood. Hated violence of any kind. A gentle soul always at odds with the wild cat he shared a body with, he fought his beast side and won, or at least kept his baser urges at bay. His only crime? He liked to gamble. Problem was he sucked at it. Not that Joey gave up. Nope, the stupid bastard. He wagered away everything he owned then went on to losing money he didn't own, which was how he ended up in jail.

But as it turned out, incarceration wasn't a bad thing. Joey finally hit his light-bulb moment in the slammer. Without the lure of gambling, or the threat of debt collectors, he turned to healthier pursuits. He read and studied, worked in the kitchen, found an inner peace his life lacked before. When Ricky visited him, he'd never seen his brother happier, which was why, when he received the notice Joey had killed himself, he didn't believe it. Couldn't.

"Someone murdered him," he'd accused to deaf ears.

No one believed him. It was easier for prison officials to say he'd killed himself and sweep it under the rug than admit the truth. However, Ricky couldn't let it go. Joey was his family. His only family. When he died, Ricky found himself alone, and that almost toppled him from the sane path he'd set himself on to the destructive one that almost took his life so many years ago.

Ricky fought the grief, just like he'd fought the anger that used to consume him as a teen. He channeled his emotions into the outreach program he managed. He also called in every favor he could to get someone in the shifter hierarchy to listen, to take notice that something nefarious was taking place and had claimed the life of one of their own. It took months, but finally someone listened and offered him a chance to help catch the culprit.

A chance for vengeance.

"We need you to go undercover. Infiltrate the prison as an inmate and see what you learn."

Piece of cake. Ricky knew the talk. Walked the walk. And he could protect himself without resorting to his inner cat. Full of cocky confidence, he'd strutted into the prison in his bright orange jumpsuit, ready to catch the perpetrator even if the chances of him being in the right prison to do so were one in who-knew-how-many.

Such grand dreams and ideals. Such good intentions. Such a crock of idealistic shit.

It took him awhile, what with him being a stubborn bastard, but even he couldn't deny he was getting nowhere. For weeks now, he'd lived and breathed prison life. He'd uncovered drug rings, fight clubs, crooked guards, slutty ones. He knew who was fucking who and who was scamming who. Met the two other shifters interspersed among the incarcerated humans. But, no one had an inkling that a faceless killer stalked them. No one had heard even so much as a whisper about the murders.

Frustrated didn't even come close to describing his emotions.

In the meantime, while he'd integrated himself here, a shifter had died in another federal prison, one that didn't have an undercover agent, which left them with only a half-dozen prisons not yet hit and a sudden increase in the odds that his temporary home might be next.

The shifter council didn't want excuses. They wanted results. To Ricky's annoyance, they decided to bring in more help. Not only was his fake lawyer who acted as his outside liaison being replaced by some chick who would be posing as a guard, they were pairing him with a shifter, some techno geek that he was supposed to protect.

Great. Just fucking peachy. Relegated to prison babysitter for a wet-behind-the-ears nerd. Much as he might dislike it, though, he'd do it. If that was what it took to bring his brother's killer to justice—a demise he intended to mete out with his bare fists—then he'd do it.

In this one instance, despite the fact he'd spent the last ten years fighting his past and the violence he used to revel in, this one instance, he would allow it, for Joey.

Chapter Four

Joking about going to prison was one thing, actually setting foot in one, a completely different thing. Stu couldn't help a twinge of unease as he shuffled along the first of many gray corridors, the tether between his ankles keeping his steps short while his hands cuffed in front of him left little movement if he stumbled and fell.

Chris would have said his face could use some character, but Stu preferred his nose as it was, only slightly misshapen from his numerous mishaps, usually at the other end of someone's fist. Ignoble tripping and a subsequent nose break wasn't the kind of scar he wanted to live with, or explain. Not when he knew it would end up repeated at every family gathering for the next twenty years. *What happened to Stu's nose? Oh, he tripped over his big freakn' clown feet and did a face plant on concrete.*

Shuffle, shuffle. He used mincing steps to keep from overbalancing, the chain jingling as he marched toward his new room and his first foray into a mission that could end in his demise if he wasn't careful. In here, there was no chance for a reboot, unlike one of his video games.

I really should have asked Patricia more questions when I had the chance. Distracted by the lovely cougar's presence in the close confines of her car, he'd not asked half the questions he should have, such as, how they expected him to ferret out information when none of their experts could. How they planned to keep him safe other than pairing him with an ex-con. Oh, and how he'd keep from drooling over the lovely Patricia every time he saw her because, idiot that he was, he'd not broached the whole, "Hey, I think you're my mate" topic. Probably because she didn't give any kind of sign she felt the same chemical attraction.

He'd have plenty of time to plan his speech to her about it now. The sparse cells certainly didn't boast much in entertainment. No television. No books. And, sob, no game consoles. He could only hope his World of Warcraft buddies didn't ditch him during his absence—or steal all his equipment!

Shuffle. Shuffle. The ignoble march wasn't as fun in person as it was to watch on television. And orange? Definitely not his color. He also wondered if he shouldn't have gotten a haircut, given the number of wolf whistles aimed his way along with catcalls of "Hey good looking, I'll be tasting your cooking", and that was one of the nicer things he heard. The one involving grease, a fist, and his poor ass … He shuddered.

They finally reached his new home. Cell block 4F. And, look, there was his new boyfriend, leering through the bars. *Reformed my ass.* The guy could have posed as the poster child for the picture under criminal element. Close-cropped hair, tattoos up and down his arms and across his hairless chest. Latino in heritage judging by his tanned skin, dark hair, and eyes, with a nose broken so many times it would never set straight. *And I'm supposed to trust him to protect me?*

As if enjoying Stu's obvious balking at

entering the cell, the other man pursed his lips and whistled. "Hey, *puta*. Come to padre."

If it weren't for the strong scent of feline, Stu would have really wondered if he was in the right place. As it was, the guy seemed entirely too immersed in his role as eager cellmate and suitor. The blown kisses and hip thrust were totally uncalled for. Stu dragged his feet, really, really wishing he'd given this more thought.

"Y-y-you know what, I've changed my mind. I don't th-think I should be here," he stammered.

"Tell someone who fucking cares," retorted his accompanying guard. With impersonal hands and rough shoves, he divested Stu of his chains and thrust him into his room, right into the arms of his partner.

The cat didn't immediately let him go but rather pulled him closer, probably so he could whisper, "Follow my lead, puppy chow, or you'll be considered fresh meat for every asshole in this place."

Lead? What lead?

A hand grabbed his ass and squeezed as his cellmate exclaimed aloud, "Nice cushion, bitch. Here's to hoping you got a set of pipes to go with that fat ass, eh?"

What. The. Fuck.

First off, his ass was not fat. Secondly, playing a role or not, touching of said ass was going a tad too far. Stu shoved and loosened the grip holding him. He stumbled back sputtering, "Keep away from me you pervert." Hmm, okay, so he was having a hard time playing along. Apparently, his reaction was the right one because his roommate never lost his salacious leer.

"The name's Ricky, *puta*. Learn it. Love it. Because you'll be screaming it later when I sink balls deep into you."

All his growled, "Hell no," earned him was a chuckle, not just from his cellmate, but the guard who'd lingered to watch their exchange.

With a rap of his baton on the bars and a laughed, "Have fun getting your ass cherry popped," the guard wandered off, leaving him alone with his partner.

Stu clung to the back wall and eyed Ricky. If he'd not known he was on his side, or so Patricia said, he would have never guessed. The guy looked like bad news.

"You get bottom bunk," the cat announced as he swung himself onto the top. "Lights will be going out in about fifteen minutes, so if you gotta piss or anything else, do it now. Or not. But, if you miss the toilet 'cause it's dark, you're cleaning it up."

"Any more fabulous advice?" Stu couldn't help the caustic edge as the reality of his situation bitch slapped him.

"Don't act too tough because otherwise you will be called on it."

"I thought we were supposed to be on the same side."

"We are, which is why I'm giving you some friendly advice. You're in the big house now, puppy. Different rules apply here. While you might be used to people following the laws outside of here, or to having your pack protect you, in here, you're a newbie. Fresh meat. You can't rely on your wolf to protect you. No one's here to back you up if someone decides they don't like your face."

"I can hold my own." Four brothers and an even more violent sister had made sure of that.

"The boys in here, they don't play by the rules. If they come after you, they won't take turns. They'll do it as a gang, and they might not stop when you cry uncle."

"Isn't it your job to protect me?"

"If I'm around. Which is why, when I'm not, it's important they believe you're already claimed."

"Claimed?"

"That you're my bitch." Ricky leered at him

"Can't we just be good friends?"

"Listen, puppy. I get that you don't understand how things work, so let me give it to you in a nutshell. In here, you've got one of a few choices. You either belong to someone as a bottom, you're part of a gang who'll keep you safe, or you're the baddest asshole around."

"And how do you get to be that last option?"

"You walk up to the meanest bastard in the place and make him cry for his momma."

"And who would that be?"

"You're talking to him, puppy."

Figured. Shit. As Stu settled onto the stiff foam mattress with its scratchy wool blanket, he really had to wonder what the hell kind of mess he'd volunteered for. What had sounded like a grand adventure and a chance to spend time with his cougar and impress her was starting to resemble a clusterfuck of mega proportions.

It galled Stu to even consider playing the part of simpering or cowed prison girlfriend to anyone, but even he recognized that as big and tough as he was, he doubted he could take his new roommate. Older, thicker, and definitely meaner, yup that about summed up his new friend and Stu didn't doubt for a moment the guy could wipe the floor with him.

But not before I got a few good licks in.

However, he wasn't here to prove himself big man in prison, and he wouldn't be giving his ass to anyone in reality. Surely he could play the part. Get the job done. Help catch the killer if they lurked in this prison and have Patricia look at him with something other than exasperation.

He clung to that hope as the lights went out—and clenched his ass cheeks tight.

Chapter Five

After ditching the wolf at the station, Patricia didn't see Stu again for three whole days. Three days she spent thinking about him, much to her annoyance.

Why did he attract her? It couldn't be the mate bond. She refused to believe that. So what was it? Surely not lust? For one thing, the guy was young, much too young. And two, she didn't like guys with wild mops of hair. She preferred a military-style cut. A groomed man. Heck, if she were to get picky, she'd admit she tended to gravitate to men in uniform.

Stu was nothing of the sort. A slob who lived with his parents and who spoke in ribald jests, whose family was borderline psychotic, who … wouldn't leave her thoughts no matter how hard she tried.

Sigh.

When she began her shift at the prison, she fought not to rush to his cell to check on him. She wouldn't be that girl. *I am a grown woman. I will act like one!* Stating that to herself and feeling it, though, were two different things. She couldn't stop the tiny thrill of anticipation as she wandered the hall that would take her past his cell. Couldn't stop the heat pooling between her thighs, the way her heart beat faster, how she stumbled to a halt when she reached the cell and met a dark-eyed gaze. The fixed stare of a predator. The flare of awareness. A tingle multiplied by two when Stu came to stand beside the man she'd previously only known via reports. A man that her cougar screamed with almost maniacal glee was also her mate.

No way.

Not two.

Two shifters.

Two mates.

Not bloody possible.

Not freakn' happening.

Pissed, she dragged her baton more harshly than she meant across the bars, rapping their knuckles. Stu grimaced and removed his hands. The other shifter just stood there. Ricky, a nickname for a boy, not the tougher than nails man standing before her. His lip curled and his eyes shone with challenge, daring her to hit him again.

"What you looking at?" she snarled, not even attempting to mask her displeasure at her cat's insistence that the two men in the cell belonged to them.

Ricky emitted a rumbling sound that sent shivers dancing over her skin. "Look at what the gods gifted me with today. A hot cougar. Me-fucking-ow. Wanna scratch me with your claws, *bebe?*"

A sneer twisted her mouth. "You wish." She lied. Despite having just met him, she did want to scratch and bite and … do utterly naughty things with him. With his tanned skin, a smooth expanse of temptation on display, given he wore his jumpsuit only to his waist, and exposing his muscled, tattooed chest, she could only too easily imagine raking nails across his back while he thrust into her with hard, savage strokes. It didn't take a genius to see this was one guy who wouldn't softly seduce, but take. Fuck her hard. And …

He gripped the bars and pressed his face to them. "Is that a dare?"

She could see his feline lurking beneath his ardent gaze. Watching her. Hungering. It roused her own beast, which she didn't appreciate. "We're not here to play games."

"Who says I'm playing? And just so you know, if I were, I'd win. I always win."

If Ricky thought he'd throw her off balance with his innuendos and his alpha version of flirting he was in for a surprise. "Don't screw with my patience. You might not like the result."

"What you going to do? Beat me with your stick? I'd like to see you try." Ricky's cocky smile needed wiping.

"I've got better ideas for your ass," she purred.

"Do tell."

"First, I tell the warden that another inmate saw you swallow something suspicious, then haul your tanned ass to the infirmary for an old fashioned charcoal cleansing followed by a water enema."

Well that wiped the smirk from his face, but only for a moment. "I could stand to lose a few pounds. This lack of exercise has made me put on weight."

Men! Did they ever take anything seriously? Almost growling in annoyance, she tore her gaze away, only to meet the soft brown one belonging to the other bane of her existence. "You got something to say, puppy?"

"The food sucks. Any chance of getting some *pie?*" Stu arched a brow.

On the surface, it sounded so innocent until one noted the heat in his eyes and the bulge below his waist. He might act more subtle and shy, but Stu was just as tempting in his own way. The jerk.

"Cry me a river," she snapped before rattling her baton across their bars and wandering away, lest anyone get suspicious about the amount of time she spent there.

But no distance could halt the stunning discovery that it wasn't just Stu setting off her mate spidey sense, but now the reformed thug known as Ricky.

Is this it? Have I hit my midlife crisis? Have I lost my marbles? Or is this some cougar version of menopause a few years earlier than expected?

Whatever it was, she wouldn't give in. Women her age did not consort with boys. And they most definitely did not mate with them.

Now if someone would only make sure her determined cougar and aroused pussy got the memo.

Chapter Six

"Holy fuck," Ricky muttered as he watched the heart-shaped ass of his mate as she strutted away. No doubt. No mistake. The blonde cougar was his. He'd seen enough of his friends and family succumb to the mysterious mating force to know what all the symptoms in his body meant.

The lady with attitude would belong to him. Fucking awesome.

"Stop staring," growled the dog who shared the cell with him.

"Don't you talk to me like that," Ricky snarled, whipping around. "I'll stare if I like, considering it's only a matter of time before that ass is mine."

"Like hell. She's my mate, and you are not laying one stinking freakn' paw on her."

"Your mate?" Ricky laughed. "You must be mistaken, puppy. The cougar is mine."

"No."

"Yes."

"No." Stu shook his head. "Can't be. Not again."

"What do you mean not again? Not the first time your pathetic nose led you astray?" Ricky sneered.

"No. My nose knows what it smells, and Patricia is mine. But my family seems to be under a bit of a curse in that my sister and a few of my brothers have multiple mates."

"Say what?"

"Ever heard the term threesome?"

"Of course. Who hasn't? Two girls, one guy, lots of fun."

"Yeah, well, it's not always two girls. My family of late seems to have an issue of the mating bond extending to two guys one girl."

Ricky practically recoiled. "Like hell. I ain't sharing my woman with another guy."

"Welcome to the club. So you won't mind stepping aside."

Ricky shook his head. "No way, puppy. That cougar is mine. You'll just have to go wagging your tail in some other bitch's face. This one is taken."

"I saw her first."

"But never claimed her. Something I'll be taking care of as soon as possible."

"Like hell you will."

"And who will stop me?"

Stu, usually easygoing, stood up to his full six foot plus height and took on a hulking appearance. Hot damn, the wolf had balls after all. But Ricky had claws and years of street experience.

"Don't push me," he warned quietly. "You won't like what happens."

"Ditto."

"How's about I get you a stuffed kitty instead when we get out? Something you can cuddle with at night. Or use as a chew toy."

"Fuck you."

"Ooh big words from a little dog."

"Little?" Stu laughed. "That's not what they say in the shower room."

Things might have escalated at that point if the bell signalling lunch hadn't gone off.

"We'll be talking about this later," Ricky promised.

"Nothing to discuss. Patricia is my mate whether you like it or not."

We'll see about that.

Ricky had often wondered if his years thumbing his nose at the law and behaving in general like a Class A asshat might have forced fate to look the other way when it came to a mate. The cougar was proof, in his mind at least, that fate had forgiven him. He'd finally earned the right to enjoy a bit of happiness. Hell, he could even think of having a family, something he'd thought would be denied him until now.

Did he plan to share that future with some smelly dog? Over his dead fucking body. The pup was probably mistaken. Letting his dick do the thinking.

And if he wasn't? What if they were both supposed to mate the cougar? Not totally unheard of in shifter circles given their numbers, but rare enough to give pause. Could he handle it? Handle seeing another man touch and kiss the woman he claimed as his own?

The growl of his cat went unheard in the stomp and shuffle of feet as they marched to the cafeteria. But, he couldn't quite bottle the covetous rage.

If the jealousy proved too much and he killed the pup, at least he already knew he could handle life in prison. *I wonder if Patricia would be open to conjugal visits?*

Chapter Seven

During the course of her shift, Patricia wandered by her charges' cell a few times, and each time, she got the same electric thrill. Heck, she found herself holding her breath in anticipation, releasing it only when she glimpsed them, each time looking yummier than the last.

She welcomed the respite in midafternoon that saw her patrolling the prison yard as a group of inmates were given their daily dose of exercise and fresh air. The change of scenery, though, didn't help, not when she realized her two guys—*my* mates— were in the group currently wandering the cement courtyard.

She did her best not to stare. It wouldn't do to draw unneeded attention to them. Yet, she couldn't help it, especially when Stu drew the scrutiny of a big, tattooed thug who stood over her young wolf, blocking the rays of sunlight Stu was trying to soak up.

With her enhanced hearing, she had no problem hearing the conversation.

"You're in my spot," growled the bald inmate.

Stu cracked open an eye and drawled, "Find another."

Patricia bit her tongue lest she mutter aloud, "Idiot." Even she knew better than to antagonize a brute flanked by a pair of bullyboys.

"Someone has a death wish," the big one said with a smirk.

"Yeah, you do since you're obviously bothering me, even though my handsome hunk of a boyfriend is standing right behind you." Stu adopted a fake, simpering smile that almost made Patricia laugh. The only thing that stopped her was the fact that Ricky did stand there, a glowering expression darkening his features.

"Do you need another lesson, Bruno?" Ricky asked in a quiet, yet, she'd wager, deadly tone.

Bruno stiffened before turning around. "Someone needs to learn how to keep their bitch in line."

"Is that so?" Ricky smiled, a cold grin that never reached his dark eyes. "Funny, because, from where I'm standing, it looks more like someone needs to be reminded not to touch what's mine."

"Kick his ass … *baby*." Stu batted his lashes, and Patricia had to cover her mouth and pretend to cough, especially when Stu caught her eye and winked.

The little devil. He knew she watched, and he did it on purpose. Did he truly not grasp he'd just lit the fuse to a powder keg?

Events exploded.

The bald inmate swung at Ricky as his buddies rushed in from the sides to hold him. But they'd not counted on Stu. While Ricky blocked the shot and began pummelling the aggressor, her wolf, with an agility she would have doubted given his joking demeanor, took out the backup. One attacker he tripped and sent sprawling, while a well-placed uppercut made the other reel.

Hopping around like a bunny on speed, Stu

then proceeded to kick their asses while making ribald jests as Ricky took down the almost seven-foot behemoth. As for the rest of the inmates? They cheered. Entertainment, especially of the violent sort, was always welcome.

It was practically a choreographed fight club comedy the way the two men handled the prison bullies with ease.

The guards did nothing to stop the fight. On the contrary, she saw money exchange hands as they wagered on the outcome.

Typical.

All too soon, the fight was over. Baldie and his friends lay bleeding and bruised on the ground while a grinning Stu jogged in a circle, hands up, humming "We Are the Champions". Ricky shook his head, wiped a bead of blood from his lip and, without warning, shot out a fist. It connected with Stu's jaw and sent the wolf to the ground.

TKO.

Now Patricia acted.

"Break it up!" she hollered, brandishing her baton, not that anyone dared touch her or even come close, not with the guns trained on them from the ramparts. While inmates could smack each other around, guards were off limits.

"Hey, *bebé*. Come to reward the winner?" Ricky angled his hips and made come-hither gestures with his fingers. He leered as well while his smoldering eyes raked her body, the heat in them intense enough to evoke an answer.

Treacherous body, it responded with her nipples tightening into aching buds. "I've got a reward for you all right," she growled. "Pick up your cellmate. You're coming with me."

"Oooh. Alone time. I like it," Ricky purred as he knelt on one knee and tugged the unconscious Stu onto his broad shoulder.

"We're going to the infirmary, dumbass," she snapped. "Then the warden's office. You can explain to him why he shouldn't place you both in solitary."

"If solitary means alone time with you, then I'll go happily," Ricky said loud enough for the watching crowd to hear. And hear they did, tittering and shouting ribald suggestions.

The man played his part of inmate all too well. Patricia stalked behind them as she prodded them on a circuitous route to the infirmary, not because they needed it but to get a few moments alone with them to talk.

"What the hell was that about?" she hissed, trying to keep her eyes off Ricky's tight ass.

Stu, who it seemed played possum, lifted his head and gave her a lopsided grin. "Just playing our part of star-crossed lovers. What do you think? Did they buy it?"

She snorted. "What happened to keeping your head down and playing it cool?"

This time Ricky made a rude noise. "This puppy wouldn't know subtle if it hit him upside the head with a two-by-four."

"Hey. I resent that. Although, you have to admit, being subtle so far hasn't been getting us anywhere."

"Exactly how did my kicking Bruno's ass advance our cause?" Ricky asked.

"Just doing as I was told."

"By picking a fight?" Patricia couldn't stem her incredulous tone.

"I was told during my debriefing to find a way to visit the warden's office."

"So they told you to antagonize a guy who could eat you for breakfast?"

"Not exactly. But you have to admit it worked. I'm going to see the big guy."

True. But, still, he'd neglected one key point. "So you found a way to visit the warden's office, smartass. How are you going to search it since the warden is likely to be there?"

"I'm working on it," Stu admitted. "I'm sure something will come to me."

Ricky sighed. "Much as I hate to admit it, his methods, while crude, are perfect for keeping our cover."

"Perfect if he gets a chance to actually search, otherwise he's putting himself, and you, in jeopardy for nothing." And for some reason she cared about that. She didn't want to see Stu, or Ricky for that matter, injured.

"Puppy's got more *cojones* than I would have given him credit for. As for getting rid of the warden for a few minutes, I got that covered. Just be sure when you handcuff the puppy to the chair that you don't do so for real. I'll take care of the rest."

They hit the infirmary, the smell of antiseptic strong and unpleasant to those with strong olfactory senses. Patricia stood guard while the nurse, a plain-featured woman in her thirties, swabbed and cleaned the minor abrasions and declared them not in need of observation.

Thick skulls like theirs probably rarely got concussions. Patricia almost snickered at the thought. Alone again as she led them to the warden, this time the pair of them walked on their two feet, arms shackled behind their backs with cuffs. She prodded them for intel.

"Anything to report?"

Ricky, his voice a low rumble that vibrated through her whole body, spoke first. "There are two other shifters in this place. The longest running going on eleven years, the newest less than six months. I've managed to more or less talk to them, without letting on what was going on. I got nothing."

"How do you ask them if they know of a psycho killer wandering around offing shifters without straight up asking?" Stu wondered aloud, which kind of mirrored Patricia's thoughts.

"Played the newbie card, asking if any of the guards or staff knew what we were and how they kept it a secret. Especially on full moons when the pull to change is strongest."

Anyone who morphed where humans could see was inviting instant discipline, usually of the fatal kind, from the shifter council. It also resulted in the humans getting subjected to a mind-altering drug to make them forget what they'd seen. The drugs weren't something anyone liked to use given the side effects were rather unpleasant for the humans involved. Not to mention there was always the fear the drug wouldn't work and they'd have to kill an innocent.

"That is a good question. What do they do? I

don't know if I can go a few weeks without shifting, let alone months or years like some of those guys." Stu made a face, and again, Patricia found her thoughts in line with Stu's. The mating bond looking for common ground or coincidence?

"Don't forget, the cells are dark at night. It's possible to let your beast out for a stretch between guard check-ins if you're careful and quiet. Also, there is someone on staff called David, a shifter like us, who apparently does his best to give us turns down in some basement area to stretch our legs and exercise our wilder side."

"And the inmates don't take advantage of this and try to escape?"

"Have you seen David?" Ricky tossed Patricia a look. She shook her head. "He makes me look small."

Given Ricky's tremendous height and size, "Holy crap!" was her only reply.

They fell silent after that as they entered an area with more human traffic. As they broached the last locked set of doors, Patricia whispered, "We're almost at the warden's. What's the plan to give Stu some time to snoop his computer?"

"Follow my lead, *bebé*. And do what I said."

With no better plan, and the opportunity to get started on their search imminent, she did as Ricky asked. When she showed the two men into the warden's office, she pretended to handcuff Stu to the metal-backed chair bolted to the floor, but before she could take care of Ricky, he lunged across the wide desk and head-butted the warden.

"I won't go to solitary," he yelled. "A man has

a right to protect himself." *Smack*. "And I demand better food!"

In between shouted demands and cries he was not at fault, Ricky banged his face against the warden's, enough times to leave the man with a bloody lip and nose. Patricia hauled Ricky off the sputtering bureaucrat.

"Filthy savage," spat the warden. "Take him to solitary while I deal with his accomplice."

That wouldn't do at all. Patricia thought fast. "But your face, sir. You really should get that taken care of first. At least some ice to prevent swelling, or you'll have a wicked bruise later. This miscreant isn't going anywhere," she pointed out.

Dabbing at his fattening lip with a tissue, the warden turned a few entertaining shades of green. "Good idea. I'll be back to mete out your punishment," the warden promised, leaving the office with a stagger.

Frogmarching Ricky, Patricia hissed over her shoulder, "Don't get caught."

Somehow she was less than reassured by Stu's ebullient, "Who me?"

Chapter Eight

Finally, a moment alone with his cougar. Of course, Ricky would have wished for a more romantic one where she wasn't shoving him down a hall with his hands pulled taut behind his back in tightly placed cuffs, but then again, he did enjoy the fact the woman fate had chosen for him wasn't some simpering wimp. He admired a woman with courage and character.

"We never were properly introduced," he stated. "My name is Ricky—"

"I know who you are. I've read the file."

And didn't sound too impressed. "Yeah. I was a bit wild in my youth."

"A bit?"

"I learned my lesson."

"You now run an outreach program to redirect teens and young adults away from gangs and into more mainstream activities. I know. Like I said, I read the file."

"It's the least I can do, given the damage I caused before I learned any better." It had taken him years to realize growing up in poverty without a father and a mother who worked three jobs did not give him license to steal, hurt people, and basically act like a jackass. Jail time, a beating by thugs who showed him he wasn't the toughest shit around, and the fatigue, not to mention disappointment in his mother's eyes, weren't the only things that helped him turn his life around. He realized he needed to stop making excuses and to clean up his act the first time the cops dragged his brother home, stoned out of his mind with pending charges for assault on a senior. His brother had attacked an old lady for her wallet so he could buy drugs and saw nothing wrong with it.

Ricky laid into him. "What is wrong with you, robbing old ladies for their pension checks?"

"What's the big deal?" his brother sneered. "You steal."

He wanted to retort he did it from people who deserved it, but the words stuck in his throat. Who made him the judge of who earned their pay check? Who gave him the right to use his strength against those weaker than him? And how could he have set such a poor example for the kid brother he'd helped raise?

"No more." Two simple words, yet he'd meant them. From that day forth, he turned over a new leaf. Ricky got a job, a shitty one washing dishes, and he began volunteering at the local outreach program. He went back to school, taking community classes to get his high school degree, and then he went on to get one in social services and sociology so he could better help and understand how to handle the kids he wanted to aid.

More than twelve years since his vow, he now split his time between his day job as a construction worker and that of a volunteer for a youth group aimed at keeping kids out of gangs.

It was hard, stressful at times, especially when dealing with some hard cases whose stories could bring a tear to even the most hardened, but he wouldn't give it up. He just wished he could have changed his path earlier in life in time to save Joey.

But Joey had chosen another path. One that led to his untimely demise.

"What you did back in the warden's office," Patricia spoke, and he snapped back to the present. "While I appreciate that you did it to give Stu a chance to go snooping, you do realize being in solitary not only puts Stu at risk without you to protect him but leaves you vulnerable to the possible attacker. Not to mention, out of the loop for intel gathering."

"I won't be in there for long. The warden's secretary likes me. She makes sure I don't spend more than a day or so in there."

"Likes you? Making *friends*, are we?" was her acerbic reply. Ricky almost grinned at the jealousy his cougar couldn't hide. So he wasn't alone in sensing the bond.

Good. It would make the next part easy. "Sheath your claws, *bebé*. She's married to my second cousin. She's going to be the one who makes sure Stu gets assigned to the library for his work detail and who will give him some passcodes to cut down his hacking time."

"First off, we're alone now, so you can drop the corny nickname. And second, this would have been useful to know before your whole attack on the warden. Had I known that, I would have never agreed to your half-assed plan."

"You wound me, *bebé*. I think that went off perfectly. The young wolf is getting a peek at our dear warden's machine, and even better, you and I get some alone time."

"Why would we need alone time?"

Play dumb, would she? Handcuffed or not, Ricky didn't hesitate to act, whipping his body around and using his size to press her up against the corridor wall out of sight of people and away from the prying gaze of surveillance cameras.

Startled, she couldn't help a gasp as her blue eyes met his. "What are you doing?"

"What I've thought of since we first set eyes on each other," he murmured, dipping his head and stealing a kiss.

A jolt of rightness, along with a tidal wave of pure lust, ripped through him. If he'd harbored any doubts, they got washed away in the rightness of the moment.

Her lips softened under his, parted even, for the thrust of his tongue. Despite his tethered hands, he managed to grind his lower parts against her. He knew she felt the hardness of his cock, smelled her erotic interest, her desire moistening her pussy and scenting the air with sweet pheromones. He growled at his inability to take things further.

"Undo my hands," he demanded in between nibbles of her lower lip.

"No."

She denied him even as she kissed him back with just as much fervor.

"I need to touch you. Claim you. Fuck you until you scream my name." He heard her breathing stutter at his words. He waited for her to comply, to release him so he could sink into her glorious heat and mark her as his.

She shoved him away, and he turned to give her his back so she could unlock his manacles.

Instead, she shoved her baton in his back and nudged him forward. "Move," she snapped.

"Looking for somewhere more private? Good plan. We wouldn't want to cause a scandal."

Reaching the solitary wing, she fumbled with the key in the lock for the door, but Ricky didn't laugh. Pride filled him at how his kiss affected her. It affected him too. It made him rage with hunger and lust and … disbelief.

She no sooner released him from his cuffs than the door slammed shut behind him, leaving him alone.

Alone? What happened to the plan to fuck until she screamed his name?

He pounded on the door. "Open this door."

She slid open the viewing slot at the top instead. Her steady blue gaze met his. "No."

"What do you mean no? I thought the plan was to finish what we started."

"You mean what you started. I realize you're chafing at the lack of female companionship, but I wasn't placed on this job so you could have someone handy to screw."

Say what? He couldn't help the arch of his brow. "Excuse me? Is that why you think I kissed you?"

"You kissed me because you were horny."

"I'd like to point out that you didn't stop me and kissed me back."

"You took me by surprise. It won't happen again."

Wouldn't happen again? Like hell. "Oh, yes, it will *bebé*. You can't stop what's happening between us."

"There is no us."

"I don't know why you're pretending when we both know we're mates, or will be once we complete the bond." Not a man to mince words, he stated it starkly.

Still she tried to deny it. "Impossible."

"What do you mean impossible? I might never have caught the mating fever before, but I've heard enough about it to know what I feel. You and I are meant for each other."

"And I say bullshit."

The vulgar word coming from her lips took nothing away from her femininity. On the contrary, he reveled in her tough side. He just wished she wouldn't use it against him.

"I can understand how you might find this all very confusing. Trust me, I was just as shocked as you when I realized it. But you can't fight destiny."

"You can when it's wrong. You're not my mate."

"How can you say that with such certainty?"

"Because I was mated before to a man I loved dearly. A mate who died. So you see, what you feel, what I feel, cannot be real. It just isn't possible."

With that final shocking claim, she slammed the viewing window shut. Not that it mattered. Rattled to his core, Ricky sat down hard on his pallet, mulling the disturbing news.

Not his mate? Absurd. The awareness, the insistence from his inner beast, the way his heart raced, how his cock reacted, the fact his whole soul vibrated when she got near screamed otherwise.

How could he be wrong? But, then again, if she'd already had a mate, then how could this be?

Perhaps fate has taken pity on my cougar and given her a second chance. Just because they'd never heard of it didn't mean it didn't happen. How to convince her though?

The swollen tingle of his lips, a remnant and reminder of her passionate reply, was his first clue.

She can deny it all she wants. She'll have to give in eventually. The fever has started. Just like a forest fire ignited in a dry forest, their need for each other would burn and consume them until they had no choice but give in to the lust. The passion. He just needed to stroke—and caress—his cougar's passion. Hunger would do the rest.

Chapter Nine

Poor Stu found nothing on the warden's computer unless the man's fetish for collecting Betty Boop memorabilia counted. Considering the male in question had run this particular establishment for the last five years and shown no indication of having traveled outside the province in all that time kind of struck him off the list of suspects. Which meant he now needed to turn his attention to everyone else on staff.

Damn. That was a lot of people to sort through.

In a stroke of luck, or on purpose, Patricia was back to escort him to his cell by the time the warden let him go with a stern warning about not getting mixed up with the wrong sort and keeping his nose clean if he wanted to earn some privileges.

Stu adopted an apologetic mien that never worked on his mother but did wonders with the warden.

"I promise to behave, sir, and to not let my roommate lead me astray."

"That's a good boy. What do you say I have my secretary sign you up for some prison work, something to keep you busy and out of trouble?"

"That sounds wonderful, sir."

It seemed Stu could act better than expected because he managed an enthusiastic smile, another promise to behave, and even earned a smile from the warden before he exited his office right into the arms of his favorite prison guard.

A grin stretched his lips. "Honey! You came back for me."

"What is it with you and your cellmate's insistence on stupid nicknames," she grumbled.

It seemed his cellmate had insisted on more than just annoying her with a pet name. Stu didn't miss the tell-tale flush in her cheeks, her slightly swollen lips, and the more telling sign of a cat having rubbed his scent all over her.

And after he'd told the irritating feline she was his mate. Back-stabbing jerk. Despite the less than ideal environ or situation, Stu would have to step up his game. Now if only he could figure out the rules along with a play that wouldn't get him tackled and penalized.

"How long is Ricky going to be gone?" Weeks if he was lucky so he could solve this case, impress Patricia, and then claim her as his own.

"A day or two, so try and keep out of trouble."

He almost pouted at her repeated insistence on treating him like a rebellious teenager. "I can take care of myself."

"But you'll be useless to me if you get yourself tossed in solitary like your friend," she reminded him.

"I'll behave."

"Somehow I doubt that."

Awww, she was getting to know him. Stu smiled. She sighed. He grinned wider. "Good news by the way. The warden likes me. Says he's going to get me assigned a job, which means a little more freedom."

"No luck I take it with his files."

"Nope. The man is clean, or at least his computer is."

"I've yet to find something on the staff," she admitted. "Then again, the RCMP only has the basics on file from their job applications. I've been running their names through Internet searches and checking out their online profiles on social sites but, so far, nothing."

"How common is it for prison staff to get transferred around to other locales?"

She shrugged. "Not very. Most people tend to stick to their hometown area to work."

"Chances are good then that we're looking for someone who would travel among prisons without drawing notice. Someone with access to prisoners and who wouldn't raise suspicions if they left after a few months, only to pop up at another one."

"Assuming they're keeping the same identity," she pointed out.

"Good point. Any chance you can sneak in some of the files from the other prisons to me?"

She snorted. "Not really. I mean, seriously, how would I explain a stack of file folders with confidential info being given to you? It's not exactly approved reading material."

"I guess not." Stu dropped his head as he pondered the dilemma. An idea struck him. "Could you put them in an online cloud and give me access? Then I'd just need to log onto a computer somewhere, say like the library, to access it."

"Do you know how long it would take me to scan all those pages?"

"Okay, maybe not the files themselves because, as you pointed out, our suspect is probably using different names, but the face would remain the same. If I could see the pictures of the staff for each prison, or have access to them online, then I could run them through some facial recognition software for comparison."

"You have access to that kind of program?"

"All good hackers do. It's why we make such good stalkers." He laughed at her mumbled, "Perv."

"Hey, I never said I did it. Just that I could." And had, if electronic stalking counted. While in the warden's office, he'd done a quick search on Patricia and gleaned some interesting information. He didn't reveal it though. Having an ace up his sleeve might come in handy.

Arriving at his cell, she ignored the catcalls of the other inmates as they passed them, but Stu frowned, and his wolf, hackles raised, growled in his mind. He didn't appreciate the lewd remarks or suggestions. This was his woman. The fact he might have once joined them in making disparaging remarks didn't mean he excused them now. Behaving himself might prove a hard promise to keep if the jerk-offs around him didn't shut the hell up.

Something in his expression must have alerted her to the fact he wasn't happy because she lowered her voice to say, "You know, if you want to call this off, let me know. I can yank you at any time. You don't have to do this."

"Why the sudden concern? Are you aware of something I'm not? Has the killer already struck?"

"No. But you got lucky today in the exercise

yard. You might not the next time. This is a human place. You can't rely on your wolf to save your skin. And I might not be around next time either. Not all the guards would step in or give a damn if some prisoner was beating your head off the cement floor."

"Then I'll have to make sure I only bother guys smaller than me."

She sighed. "Are you intentionally trying to drive me nuts?"

"I'd rather drive you insane with passion, but we don't exactly have the privacy for that."

She recoiled from him. "You're too young for me. I thought we already discussed that."

"No. You claimed it. I never agreed. If you ask me, you're just right."

"You know you're the second guy in the past week to think he's my mate."

A curl of Stu's lip went well with his caustic, "I heard about Ricky's supposed claim."

"Don't worry. I set him straight. I guess I should tell you since I already told your misguided roommate. I was mated once before."

"I know." His quiet admission had her stumbling a step back. "I also know he died a few years ago."

"You spied on me?"

"You call it spying, I call it research. I wanted to know who I was working with."

"Did your stalking also mention I'm not looking for another mate?"

"Fate doesn't always give us that choice."

"Then fate is an even crueler bitch than I gave

her credit for." Bitterness in her words and eyes shining bright with moisture, Patricia shoved him into his cell, and the door slammed shut, the click of the tumbling lock her final say on the matter.

Or so she thought.

Far from being an idiot, Stu had grasped from the moment he'd read about her previous mating in her file that she'd take some convincing. He knew many shifters believed that they could only mate once, for life. But, when first his sister then a few of his brothers ended up in polyamorous relationships, he'd studied the rules he'd grown up with and discovered a number of interesting facts.

For one, ménage groupings were not all that uncommon, especially when shifter birth levels reached all-time lows or when one sex dominated the numbers of the other. It seemed nature had a way of wanting to restore balance. He also discovered that if a mate died, then it wasn't entirely unusual, if the one left behind was still in child-bearing age, to have another mate appear on the scene.

As for Patricia's insistence that age should keep them apart ... Exactly when should he admit he'd always preferred a more experienced woman? Even as a young man, he'd eschewed the bubbly girls who flocked the clubs and singles scene for the more mature ladies who knew what they wanted. A mature woman knew how to not only ask for what she wanted but give it. They also didn't play the games or give in to the emotional crap those with less experience and maturity did. The older females also had a tendency to see past his foot-in-the-mouth syndrome and seduced him instead of ridiculing his attempts at flirting.

Given the choice between a kitten his age or a cougar like Patricia, he knew who he wanted. Now he just needed to convince her, which meant he needed a plan to get her alone. If he could only kick-start the mating fever, then nature would take care of the rest. Once she gave in to the spark growing between them, he'd leave prison a changed man. A mated one.

Chapter Ten

"Bloody fucking hell." The curse echoed in the barren room, the highlight of the place the wall plastered with prison schematics, schedules and pictures of inmates. Welcome to the war room where the hand of justice plotted its next move. And next killing.

According to the lunar calendar, the full moon approached, which meant the time to put the plan in motion was imminent. The prison, which initially boasted only two noticeable shifters, suddenly spawned two more, but in a bad stroke of luck, the newest ones shared a cell.

How to arrange an incident without a witness? Taking them both out with the drug smuggled in past oblivious guards was doable, but how believable would a dual *accident* seem? Was it time to add a new scenario to the list?

Waiting for an opportunity to strike meant letting the filthy animals live. Letting them wear a mask of humanity. Hiding amongst them, waiting for their chance to harm the unsuspecting. Something had to be done, but overreaching wouldn't achieve that goal. Sticking to the current plan would have to do for the moment. Perhaps by the time the next full moon occurred, the housing situation for the two newest shifters would have changed. Cellmates were reassigned all the time.

At least the first pair would prove easy. The lone shifter who spent most of his time staring at the walls of his cell in solitary—reports claimed he'd lost his interest in communicating years ago—would prove no issue. He would die first.

The other dirty beast on the schedule for extermination shared a cell with a human. Lucky break, the human male was currently involved romantically with a guard. By keeping a close eye with a specially placed camera, it would be simple to slip in during one of those trysts and administer justice.

And then that would leave only two. Two fit animals that would have to be split up. Difficult or not, they would die. Where there was a will, there was a way. A promise needed to be kept. Vengeance would be satisfied. And the unholy creatures walking among them would pay for what they did with their lives.

Chapter Eleven

The emptiness of the apartment taunted Patricia. Why it bothered her today when she usually treated it only as a place to sleep and eat she couldn't have said. There was nothing physically wrong with the space. It was just a generic apartment, rented because of its proximity to the prison, so similar to the one she lived in just outside of Ottawa.

Beige walls, beige carpeting, the furniture that came with the place—black pleather sofa and chair, two-person pine dinette set, a simple double mattress on a metal frame. The only thing different from this apartment versus her own was hers at least had her favorite shows on PVR.

Unsettled but unable to pinpoint why, Patricia skipped dinner—not a hard task given the frozen variety meals she kept stocked in the freezer, blech—and stripped in favor of a shower. She draped her uniform on a chair in the bedroom before heading into the bathroom, where the mirror over the sink cast her reflection. She paused to take a look.

It wasn't vanity to admit that, for a woman her age, she looked good. She kept herself in shape, working out daily, eating healthily, and it showed in the clarity of her skin, the tautness of her muscles, and general healthy appearance. Just shy of the big four oh, yet she could probably pass for early to mid-thirties. Not bad.

What bothered her was why she even pondered her looks. Could it have something to do with the fact that she had not one but two younger guys vying for her attention? Actually, they wanted more than her attention. They both outright proclaimed an interest in claiming her as their mate.

Why? Why them, why now, and the most important question of all, what should she do?

Despite the fact she'd told them it was impossible, she couldn't deny the pull they both emitted and the attraction and, yes, the interest of her cougar. It only took seeing them to make her inner kitty pace and yowl, urging her to mark the men and claim them.

Her inner feline didn't care that Patricia preferred to remain single. *That I don't want to lose or ruin my memories of Ryker.* She recognized all too well the signs of the mating fever. The hunger. The uncontrollable arousal. The need …

A part of her even welcomed the sensations, the feeling of aliveness thrumming through her. How long since she'd felt more than a passing interest in the world around her? But another part, at the same time, felt guilt. *How can I betray Ryker like this?* Never mind he would never want her to spend the rest of her life alone. She couldn't help but feel that by even thinking of the other two men she betrayed what she'd once shared with her mate. *I loved him so much.* And when he died, it was as if a part of her died with him. Only … the hole in her heart, the ache that was her constant companion these past few years, had disappeared. Something filled it. Threatened her memories.

I don't want to forget Ryker.

But what could she do to stop it, to stop Stu

and Ricky from wiping out her past? Even separated from them, she couldn't turn the tide of her thoughts. When Ricky kissed her today, she almost lost control, almost took him up on his offer to find somewhere private and ride him to ecstasy. Her body still lamented the fact she'd walked away.

Then there was Stu, even younger and shyer in his declaration. The less suave wolf had admitted his feelings and was unable to hide his hurt when she'd brushed him off. Worse? It pained her to do it. She wanted to take the words back and soothe him, kiss away his pain and …

No!

He deserved someone closer to his age. Someone less emotionally damaged. Someone cute and perky … and young.

Bitch! It wasn't just her cat who snarled at the thought of Stu with another woman. Patricia's fingertips dug into her palm hard enough to leave crescents. Hello, jealousy. Long time, no see.

Stepping into the hot shower, Patricia tipped her head back and let the warm spray sluice at her worries. It did nothing to fix her dilemma, but her muscles did relax. As she lathered soap on her body, she kept mulling her choices.

Ignore the two men – not an option. She needed to work as closely as she dared with them without giving their cover away until she or one of the other undercover groups at another prison could find the person killing shifters.

Next option, convince them, and herself, they were mistaken. Somehow she didn't think they would give up easily. Ricky seemed the type to latch on and not let go once he set his mind to something. As for Stu, she'd met his family. Stubbornness was an inherited gene. And, really, if she couldn't convince herself they weren't her mates, then how was she supposed to change their minds?

So what did that leave?

Her cat purred. Her body warmed. And her pussy, the one between her legs, clenched, sending a delightful shudder through her frame.

Take them up on their offer. Have sex with them, great sex. Enjoy myself. Feed the hunger, but … don't let them mark me. Perhaps she could keep the fever at bay by at least satisfying her bodily urges and just not take the final step. Would it work?

She didn't know. The whole prison thing would make getting any privacy for the act difficult, but on the other hand, any sex she did indulge in would be quick, and she could skip any post-coital talk or cuddling, using the excuse of secrecy.

But what about once the mission was over and they went back to their regular lives? What then?

I always did love the solitude of the Rockies.

Chapter Twelve

Ricky spent two days in solitary, two days of mind-numbing boredom without a single visit from his cougar. Disappointment became his newest friend. And he discovered even a grown man could pout. *Why is she ignoring me?* He'd not found himself able to. On the contrary, he'd spent quite a bit of those two days thinking about her. Fantasizing about what he'd do the next time he got her alone. Picturing her bent over. Atop him. Under him. How she'd feel and taste. How she'd sound when she came. How she'd smile and …

… pretend as if nothing ever happened between them when she did finally fetch him from his confinement.

When the slot in the door slid open, her scent immediately wafted through, and he couldn't help a spurt of adrenalized anticipation. His initial jolt of joy died a quick death when she curtly demanded, "Please turn around and place your hands through the hole for cuffing."

The indifference in her tone irked him. "What? No hello? How have I been?"

"I'm not here to socialize."

Someone didn't sound happy. That made two of them. "And I'm not here because I enjoy staring at four walls," he snapped.

A heavy sigh left her. "Sorry. It's been a rough few days. Hello, Ricky." Oh, how grudgingly she said it.

"Everything okay?"

"Yes. I'm just frustrated by our lack of progress. It doesn't help that I'm dealing with a-holes every day."

"Anybody I need to *talk* to?" If any of the prisoners needed an attitude re-adjustment, he was more than happy to help. No one messed with *his* woman.

"Nothing I can't handle and nothing pertinent to our case. Now that we've exchanged pleasantries, can you please place your hands outside the hole for cuffing? You do know there is a camera watching along this hall. I'd rather not have to explain why it took me so long to get you to listen. They already think I'm less than fit for the job because I'm a woman."

He slid his hands through the narrow opening in the door and felt the familiar cold metal snapped around his wrists. "If only they knew you could kick their ass."

"I've been tempted to show them," she admitted on a wry note.

Manacled, he withdrew his hands from the slot and took a few steps away from the door. He knew the drill. "I was beginning to wonder if you'd forgotten about me."

"The warden took a bit longer to convince than expected, or so your cousin's wife said."

"I was expecting you to visit me."

"I couldn't get away without causing suspicion."

Lie. Ricky could spot it, but he didn't call her on it. Apparently, his cougar seemed determined to try and ignore what had happened between them. The door creaked open, and he turned to see her looking as tempting as usual. The baton she held in a ready-to-strike position didn't faze him a bit. Tough was a good look for her. "I missed you."

She ignored his admission and did her damnedest to keep her gaze from meeting his. "Nothing weird to report?"

"I didn't see or scent another soul, other than the guards who fed me. I was bored out of my freaking skull so much that I entertained myself by catching a few rats."

Her lips twitched. "You're kidding?"

"I wish. I swear my kitty is trying to fatten me up."

She made a gagging noise. "Oh please tell me you didn't."

At her appalled expression, he burst out laughing. "Of course I didn't eat them. Once I caught them, I gave them to the guard when I passed back my food tray. You should have heard the one squeal like a pig."

Her lips twitched. "Let me guess, the fat one?"

"Seems he has a phobia."

"That was naughty."

"Very naughty. What can I say. I am a bad, *bad* boy." Ricky took a step toward her, and she shied away. He took another, and she practically tripped over her own feet to keep out of reach.

So this was how she wanted to play? Act as if he possessed the plague? Like hell. Ricky lunged, quick as an adder, but before he could try and pin her to the wall again—and steal another kiss—she sidestepped him and rapped the baton across his hip. Ouch. His cougar had some muscle and knew how to use it.

"Behave," she snapped, her irritated tone at odds with the rapid racing of her pulse.

"What if I don't want to?"

"You have to. As I said, there's a camera along this hall."

"Manned by guards who don't give a shit. You and I both know hanky-panky goes on all the time."

"We're here to do a job, not screw around like horny teenagers."

"I'm hurt. Comparing me to an unschooled boy … I'll have you know I have more finesse than that. Give me a try and you'll see."

"Or let's try and think with a head not south of our belt buckle and do what we came to do. Solve a crime. Or have you forgotten what tonight is?"

How could any shifter not know? The rising full moon tugged at him. It called to his inner beast and asked him to join it for a wild, night-time run. Usually he would heed the invitation, but given his present circumstances, he tamped down the urge. His panther grumbled. It chafed at their current lifestyle. "I know what day it is. Tonight is the night we find out if our killer has selected its next target." Because it seemed most of the deaths occurred on full moons. Was it because shifters and their odd traits were more noticeable, or was there another reason?

"I'm on the night shift for the next couple of nights. It's all been arranged. I'll be walking your floor at regular intervals to keep an eye."

"The killer won't strike while there are two of us in the cell."

"I know. Which is why Stu is going to have a medical emergency that requires me taking him to the infirmary. He should be safe there. Once he's out of the way, I'm going to swing by the cells of the other two shifters in this place. One should be okay. He's got a human roommate. But the other, he's kind of secluded in his wing."

"What about me? I'll be all alone." With a bed, a hard-on, and too many fantasies.

She pretended not to catch his hint. "Boo-freakn'-hoo. And here I took you for a guy who could protect himself."

The barb made him laugh. "I can. But it doesn't mean I wouldn't like my hand held, among other things."

Oh, she caught the innuendo that time, and the temperature between them rose a notch. "Don't start. You need to focus on the job."

"I am well aware of the stakes and what I have to do, but it doesn't mean I'm going to ignore you. Fight it all you want, *bebé*. It's only a matter of time before we end up together." A straight shooter in real life, he didn't pull any punches when it came to dealing with Patricia.

"No we're not."

"You are living in denial. Face facts. No matter what you say, or pretend, we both know in the end, I will have you. Naked. Sweating. Panting. And creaming hard. I promise you'll be purring by the time I'm done." Ricky didn't play coy. He'd already had a glimpse of her passion. The main event was sure to prove explosive.

She didn't appreciate his frankness. "How romantic. Perhaps you'd like to throw in a few more caveman statements like, 'My cock stopped breathing when you walked in the room. Wanna give it some mouth-to-mouth?' or how about 'I'm gonna crawl between your legs and eat my way straight to your heart.'?"

"Hey, I never said anything that corny."

"But you keep implying it. Just so you know, there is nothing less attractive than a man who thinks a woman's place is on her knees or her back servicing him. You should also take note that, not only do I not go for the macho type, but I also hate to cook and clean."

"You wound me. I am a modern man. I am more than happy to be a stay-at-home husband while you work and bring home the bacon. And steak. Preferably a T-bone."

"You just don't give up, do you?"

"When it comes to things I am passionate about, I am tenacious."

"I don't get it. You barely know me, and yet you're so willing to tie yourself to me, to imagine a future together. What if I'm the biggest bitch on the face of this earth? What if I snore? Or belch in public? What if I like to sing show tunes, out of key, on street corners?"

"I have faith that whatever drew us together did so because we have a chance at happiness." He could have added that she was exactly his type. Had they met outside the prison, even without the mating urge, he would have hit on her. He liked women of character who didn't simper before a man and who possessed minds and opinions of their own. He wanted someone who could engage him on all levels, not just a sexual one. But how could he convince her of that?

"I get it. You find me attractive, and you want to bang me. Sexual compatibility is not something to base a whole future on."

"And, yet, isn't that how most relationships start? First, you notice the exterior package, and your brain sends a message along the lines of 'Hey, this broad is hot.' Then your eyes meet, and there's a little spark, a shared moment where you're like, 'I want to get to know this gal.' Next thing you know, you're talking and making out."

"Or slapping the forward jerk and stomping away."

He grinned. "I think we've ascertained at this point that we're a little more compatible than that. Or have you failed to notice the fact we've been talking more than lusting?"

Her lips pursed. "I would have classed it more as arguing."

"Nothing wrong with a lively discussion."

"Fine. Split hairs and call it what you like. We still don't know much about each other as people."

"Easily rectified. I like the color blue. Bacon that's practically burnt. And I watch *Vampire Diaries*, but will deny it if asked in public. Your turn." He tossed her a challenging smile over his shoulder.

"We don't have time for this," she hissed as they entered the more populated area of the prison.

"Oh please. No one is listening to us." Nor looking for long because all it took was one scowl from Ricky to send their attention elsewhere. A reputation for being a badass was a good thing to have in prison. "So come on, *bebé*. Spill it. Favorite color and food."

"Red and cheesecake." She mumbled it, not seeming pleased at all, which was why he was surprised when she said, "I like to watch *Once Upon A Time,* even if I want to slap Snow White for being such a pansy. And if you tell anyone, I will hurt you."

He couldn't help a spurt of laughter. "Was that so hard?"

"Yes."

Further talk became nearly impossible as they entered the main area of the prison, but Ricky inwardly smiled. Maybe he'd not gotten to act out any fantasies yet, but he'd taken a step in the right direction getting her to open up, even if grudgingly.

He really did need to finagle some alone time though. Maybe tonight. If he could convince her to let him out so he could roam, under the pretext of sniffing out the killer, then perhaps he could sneak in a kiss or two or *more*. He wasn't kidding when he boasted he could make her purr. And if he was really lucky, he'd wear some scratches to prove it.

Chapter Thirteen

Patricia left Ricky in the common area and went looking for Stu. Her cougar prowled her mind, restless and displeased. It lamented the fact she'd not let the rough-around-the-edges panther claim her or, at the very least, manage a grope. While Patricia might be a modern woman who valued her freedom and choices, her inner animal was more than eager to let a man place his mark upon her.

What she saw as a crude pickup line, her beast saw as strength and determination. Much as it galled her, Patricia couldn't help but feel pleasure at his insistence he'd have her. That he wanted her. A part of her was even disappointed that she didn't get a kiss.

There's always tonight.

No. She tamped that thought right down. Tonight she needed to pay close attention to what went on. It would suck to have to explain, not to mention live with the guilt, if the killer struck on her watch. Especially if one of her guys got hurt.

They're not mine. Funny how she kept saying that to herself and, yet, believed it less and less. Every time she saw them, her resolve melted a little more. How much longer before she gave in?

On her coffee break, she went looking for her other dilemma. She came across Stu, head bent over a table in the library, tapping away at a keyboard that had seen much better days, or so the aging yellowed plastic casing indicated. Even the monitor looked ancient, its bulky size a far cry from the slim screens around today. But at least the computer itself sported some modern amenities, such as access to the network and, with the proper passcodes to get past the firewalls, the Internet.

On paper, if anyone bothered to look, the prison administrative logs had Stu working volunteer hours cataloguing the prison library from the archaic card system to a computer checkout one. In reality, he sifted the files she'd painstakingly copied over into an online cloud. The mind-numbing work, which she did at night when she left the job, helped keep some of her racier fantasies at bay—until she closed her eyes.

Then the claws came out, whatever clothes she wore in her dream state got shredded, and Patricia woke squirming, sweaty, in need of fresh sheets and a shower.

Men weren't the only ones who could experience the joys—and frustrations—of wet dreams.

As usual, Stu knew she'd arrived, but unlike Ricky, he didn't try and force her to admit things she wasn't ready for. A part of her wondered if he wished he could retract his shy declaration since he'd not referred to it or repeated it, even though she'd come around to see him a few times. He kept their interactions professional, his few fumbles into social niceties awkward, for him at least. She, on the other hand, found his inability to meet her eyes when they were alone adorable. Ugh.

"Still nothing?" she queried, leaning over him under the guise of checking out the screen. In reality, she couldn't help but inhale his scent. Mmm. Her cat practically purred in delight, and she almost forgot herself. She moved away before she nuzzled him.

"Nada." Stu leaned back in his chair with a sigh. "I can't find anybody on the employee lists who was at all the prisons. None of the names match, and according to facial comparisons, none of them are even related. I'm beginning to think, whoever the killer is, they're not working for the prison system, or at least not on the public dime."

"But who does that leave?"

He shrugged. "Private contractors. Visitors. Delivery men. Shapeshifting mice."

A snort left her. "Mice? Now you're really pushing it." She leaned her hip against the table he worked at, and his eyes finally met hers. The flare of awareness no longer shocked her, but it didn't diminish either. Nor could she help the spurt of heat between her legs when his lips curled into a smile.

"Okay, so maybe not mice. But someone is managing to slip under the radar in all these places. Someone who is succeeding in gaining access to cells, even late at night, without setting off alarms."

"Each of the prisons handles security a little differently. Some, like this one, still use keys, but others have gone to electronic keypads. Have we traced the codes used during those windows to see who accessed those areas?" she mused aloud.

"First thing I checked. In the cases where logs were kept, it was off-duty guard codes used. In one prison, the one where the killer got to five, he used five different codes."

She zeroed in on one word. "You said he.

How sure are we that the suspect is a man?"

Stu frowned. "It seems logical. Most serial killers are male."

"Most, but not all."

"Okay, I'll give you that one, but you're also talking about someone capable of killing full-grown men. Not just men, but shifters. No offense, but not many women could take one on and win."

"But the victims were drugged."

"I hardly see them standing still to get injected."

"You found proof of a needle?"

Stu whirled around and tapped, pulling up an autopsy report. "Back of the neck, a tiny pinprick."

She perused the file. "Is that the only victim showing that mark?"

"Yes, but then again, no one was looking for signs of foul play initially."

"Which makes my theory of a woman even more possible. Think of it." Patricia pushed away from the desk and paced. "A female, maybe one who's befriended the guards outside the prison, gets the codes. She slips in and jabs them with a needle. Then, when they're incapacitated, kills them."

A moue creased his face. "That's weak. I mean first off, having the codes for inside the prison doesn't get her past the gate. What's her excuse for visiting late at night? Secondly, if she's just dating a guard, then how does she know who the shifters are? I mean, even another shifter couldn't tell unless they got close enough to smell them."

Patricia sat back on the edge of the table. "Way to shoot my theory down."

"If it's any consolation, I like how you're thinking outside the box. It never even occurred to me to look for a female attacker. That opens up a whole new can of worms."

"It does? How?"

"Thus far, I've concentrated on males on staff."

"Misogynist," she coughed.

He laughed. "Guilty. I'll admit the idea of a woman serial killer is a hard one for me to grasp. But your reminder of the date rape drug, and my finding of the puncture wound, they throw it into a whole new light. And it opens up a huge pool of suspects. Secretaries, kitchen staff, nurses, dental hygienists."

"Nuns."

"Nuns?" He snorted. "Those little old ladies?"

"Think again. Many an abused or emotionally shattered woman has turned to god regardless of their age."

Stu frowned. "I'm really going to have to expand my search parameters."

"Expand them later. I need to get you back to your cell before lights out."

"But, if you just give me a—"

She placed her hands atop his to stop him from typing. Problem was, while he froze his motions, something else chugged to life. Awareness. Passion. Need. Call it what you would, it burst into existence. Their eyes met, their gazes locked. She couldn't have said who moved first. Her. Him.

It didn't matter. One moment they were sitting, the next, they'd moved as if possessed of one mind out of sight of the camera. In their little corner of privacy, they clung to each other, lips meshed in a panting kiss that set her nerve endings on fire.

Where Ricky was hard all over—lips, body, even his fingers—Stu was softer, not weak soft, but more sensual, hesitant. She was the aggressor, the one in control. Her fingers tangled in his strands and locked him in place for her to plunder his mouth. She was the one pressing her body against his, revelling in the pulsing of his cock against her lower belly, making a soft moan of encouragement when his hands came to hesitantly rest on her hips.

"Touch me," she encouraged despite her previous vows to remain aloof. What had fighting her body done for her? Nothing but make her crabby and miserable.

For two days, she'd fought the urge to touch and caress. For two days, she'd argued against taking things any further, of showing any encouragement. Like a dam being pressed by a raging river, she burst. She no longer possessed the will to control herself. She let the current of her passion sweep her away.

The tip of her tongue eased past his lips and engaged in a teasing slide across his. The fingers just below her waist dug in, and he ground himself against her, growing bolder. She nipped his bottom lip with her teeth, and he gasped. Without realizing she moved, she pressed him against the wall of the library, unheeding of the fact someone could come across them. She really didn't give a damn at the moment. She wanted more of Stu. And she took what she wanted.

Tearing at the Velcro enclosure at the front of his jumpsuit with rough fingers, it opened enough for her to slide a hand down the front. His cock sprang eagerly into her hand, thick and hot. She pumped it, and she swallowed his groan with her mouth as she smeared the pre-cum on the tip of his cock.

"For a shy guy, you're packing some impressive heat," she murmured against his lips.

"Maybe that's my problem. Not enough blood left in my brain when a gorgeous woman gets her hand on me," he quipped.

"If this is how it gets for a hand, then what if I embrace it with something else?"

"Here? Now?" His voice rose an octave, and a shudder went through his body.

"Yes now," she purred. Nipping at his jaw, she followed the line of his throat, kissing her way down his chest, revealed by the open vee of his jumpsuit.

"But—but, what if someone walks in." He gasped as she sucked at the tender flesh around his naval.

"Good point." Standing abruptly, she grabbed a chair and, making sure to stay out of sight of the camera, wedged it under the knob of the only door into the room. Secured, and guaranteed some privacy, she turned to him with a hungry, slightly predatory, smile.

Her young wolf couldn't help his nervous swallow or hide the excitement in his dilated pupils. He didn't move as she stalked back to him, hips swaying in a hypnotic fashion that drew his gaze. She raked her nails down his furred chest, emitting a husky chuckle when he sucked in a ragged breath. Down further, she scraped the tips of her fingers. His flesh pimpled in reaction, his senses ultra-aware of her every motion.

His jumpsuit parted farther as she slid both hands into his outfit, fist over fist, clasping the hard shaft waiting for her. He let out a groaned, "Yes, oh yes."

Still coherent? She'd have to change that. Releasing her grip on him, she grabbed at his jumpsuit and pushed it down over his arms so that it draped at his waist. Dropping to her knees, she brought herself eye level with his groin, and she couldn't help an impatient lick of her lips as she tugged the fabric hiding his dick.

The jumpsuit pooled around his ankles, revealing him in all his naked glory. Shy and geeky did not mean small and puny. Stu might prefer to spend his time in front of a computer screen, but his body didn't show it. While somewhat stocky and less fit than Ricky, he nevertheless had a nice build to him, a solid body from his thick thighs and wide chest to his jutting long and fat cock.

"What do we have here?" she teased, gripping him with one hand and stroking his length. "Someone seems a little happy to see me."

"I'd hardly say little," he managed to utter in a low mumble.

Her laughter blew warm air on his shaft, and it jumped, responding to even that slight stimulation. "No, not so little. I wonder if it will fit. What do you say we try and see?" He didn't reply to her teasing, unless his garbled "unnnh" counted.

The smooth skin of his cock made gliding her hand along it much too easy. The heat, though, oh my the heat rising from it just about scorched her palm. A quick peek up found him gazing down upon her with wonder and lust. His eyes practically smoldered. The intensity roused something in her and made her own body heat in response. Their eyes locked and she couldn't help a half smirk as she stuck out her tongue and ran it around his swollen head, the pre-cum on the tip a salty flavor for her taste buds. Down the ridge of his cock she swiped her tongue, letting out a pleased growl when he swallowed hard while the cords on his neck stood out in sharp relief. Oh, how he fought to stay in control. Did he not realize he wouldn't win this battle? Much like a kitty with a yummy bowl of cream, she lapped at him, enjoying every inch of his cock before she took him fully into her mouth, engulfing him in warmth and wetness.

Back his head went, unheeding the wall behind it, which he hit with a solid thump. It didn't seem to affect him in the slightest because his cock remained plump between her lips. Pleased at his reaction, she worked him, lips sliding back and forth, her hand gripping the base and squeezing in rhythm. Until now, his hands had remained clenched at his side, but as if finally feeling comfortable enough, or with a need stronger than his hesitation, his fingers tangled themselves in her hair. She moaned her approval, and the grip tightened, and when he helped her bob his dick in and out of her wet orifice, she couldn't help but purr, a sensuous rumble, which he surely felt.

"Ohmyfuckinggod," he moaned. His pleasure rendered him practically incoherent. But would he lose control? She inhaled hard, sucking his dick, pulling at it, working it, delighted at his sobbing of her name. At least he knew who to thank.

It would have been so easy to let him come in her mouth, to finish him off, but Patricia discovered she possessed a selfish side. A hungry side that wasn't content to let him have all the fun.

For once, a man was the one to mewl in disappointment when she pulled away from his cock, but he soon caught on the fun wasn't done.

It didn't take much for her pants to end up around her ankles, but they both lacked the patience to remove her boots so she could step out of them. The fact her thighs could only spread a short distance added an element of daring to the act. With her hands braced on the wall, she thrust her buttocks back and tossed a coy glance over her shoulder, smiling at Stu's glazed look and then creaming herself as she saw him gripping his cock and keeping it primed.

"Planning to use that thing?" she teased.

"Are you sure?"

Ah, how sweet. How gentlemanly. How annoying. She didn't want words. She wanted action.

In a low growl, she demanded, "Fuck me and quickly, would you? We haven't got all night." Despite her impatience, throwing caution to the wind didn't mean she didn't remain partially aware that their situation wasn't exactly private. What if someone noticed they hadn't checked in? What if she'd miscalculated about the camera? What if it panned wider than expected? Oh god, someone could be watching them at this very moment. "Stu!"

It wasn't begging, not entirely, more of a command to stop staring and screw her.

Aroused beyond belief, she came a little when his hard cock finally probed her wet slit, a spasm of muscle that had her scraping her nails against the wall. He eased into her with an aching slowness that almost made her scream. Bit by bit, he stretched her, filled her, drove her insane.

Her pussy clenched tight, and he gasped. "Oh fuck."

Oh fuck was right. She couldn't help but shudder around his dick, squeeze him tight with her channel, which resulted in him swelling. His increased size pushed at her, and his fingers dug into the bare flesh of her hips. Back she pushed against him, wiggling and silently demanding he give her more. His grip tightened. He thrust in farther, seating himself to the hilt, and now it was her turn to release a breath.

All hesitation left him as he pulled back and slammed back in.

"That's it." She panted, trying to regain control of the situation. "Give it to me hard."

He practically lifted her right off her feet so hard did he thrust. She grunted, and he paused.

"Did I hurt you?"

So much to teach him. She turned her head to peer at him over shoulder. "The only thing that hurts is the fact I haven't come yet."

She caught the bruising kiss he placed upon her lips, a fiery embrace that stole her breath. As he slammed in and out of her, she kept her hands braced against the wall, welcoming his savage thrusts, his loss of control. He even grew bold enough to let his hands roam her body. His fingers reached under and found her clit. He paused in his pumping to rub her, and she couldn't help but squirm. Couldn't help but cry out. Couldn't help but have a pre-orgasm, which sent ripples along her sex and squeezed his cock.

But she wanted the big O. "Stop screwing around," she growled. "And finish it."

H resumed his slamming cadence, seesawing his cock in and out, filling not only her pussy but a lonely void within her, satisfying her in a way she'd thought to never feel again. Clenching tight around him, she rode the wave to ecstasy, all the while ignoring the spinning of her cat that demanded she do more. *Claim him,* her feline begged. *Mark him, screw him, take him, and keep him as our own.*

But even amidst the passion, Patricia held back, not ready for that step. But not ready to commit didn't mean she was going to deny herself the pleasure Stu wanted to give, not when it felt so freakn' good.

Together they gyrated, her legs tethered by her slacks, the tight space making for short, deep thrusts, but they were enough, enough to have her shuddering and panting, to have her sex spasming and tightening. When her orgasm hit, she bit her own arm to muffle her scream, the pain not enough to detract from the pleasure.

Panting and grunting, Stu wasn't far behind, and she could have kissed him when he had the presence of mind to pull out just before he came, creaming her lower back.

"Sorry about the mess," he said in a tone that screamed embarrassed. "I didn't know what else to do."

"I've got tissues in my pants pocket."

Stu bent to scrounge in her pocket and, moments later, swiped at the signs of his passion. Their passion. As the tremors in her body died down, the reality of her actions set in.

Good god. What have I done? Had amazing sex for one. But with Stu, a guy almost ten years her junior. Never mind it blew her mind and he'd wanted it too. She'd done it, and not just done it, but also done it while on the job—and, more unforgivable, loved it.

Guilt made her voice harsh when she ordered, "Get dressed. You need to go back to your cell."

In silence they dressed, with her cowardly avoiding the questioning glances he kept shooting her way. She said not a word to him as she cuffed his hands behind his back and led them from the library.

What could she say?

That was fucking amazing. By the way, we can never do it again because I'm afraid next time I won't be able to stop myself from claiming you. He wouldn't understand why she found the thought so abhorrent. So, she pretended to be her distant cousin the Cowardly Lion and said nothing at all.

Chapter Fourteen

Color him confused. Stu could feel the anger radiating at his back and couldn't figure out the reason. Patricia acted as if he'd done something terrible, and yet, he'd not been the one to initiate their lovemaking. Enjoyed it, yes, but given his cougar's history and their current location, he'd made a vow to himself to keep things on the down-low for as long as possible—even if it hurt, which it most assuredly did, giving new meaning to the term blue balls. More like purple.

His vow to behave, though, didn't mean he didn't harbor the hope they'd solve the case quickly and re-enter the real world, where he could woo Patricia properly. Hopefully with pointers from his more suave brothers—whom he'd have to bribe into secrecy, maybe with threats to ruin their credit rating or post little dick pics online. With his future and love life at stake, he could admit he needed help when it came to the fairer sex. Major help.

Resigned to a torturous wait, imagine his surprise when, out of nowhere, she practically attacked him, a welcomed sensual attack, but still, she'd started it! And only an idiot would have taken the high road and not helped her finish it. He'd totally enjoyed it, thought she had too but, for some reason, he now seemed to be in the doghouse because of it.

I'll be the first to admit I don't understand women, but this takes the cake. He didn't think he'd done anything wrong. She came. He knew she did, there was no mistaking the incredible sensation of her sex spasming around him. Hell, he almost went cross eyed thinking about the wondrous moment. So it wasn't a lack of orgasm making her mad. He hoped. *Because if she didn't come, then I've really been fooling myself when it comes to women and sex.*

He sifted through the events of the past half hour. He'd not insulted her. He'd not forced her into anything. She'd come on to him, and he'd responded, enthusiastically. He could check orgasm off the list. He'd achieved that portion, even she couldn't fake the convulsive squeeze of her sex. No blood or screaming which meant he'd not inadvertently hurt her, although he couldn't discount a possible charley horse, which could account for her sudden foul mood.

Despite the urge, and his wolf's insistence, he hadn't marked her in any way, even though he wanted to so freakn' bad. He even pulled out before coming, conscious that not only did he not wear a rubber, but that coming inside her might have the same effect as a mating bite. Or so he'd read. Views on what constituted an actual claiming differed. Some said an exchange of bites needed to occur. Others that a man need only spew his seed inside a female to make his claim.

Stu held off on both accounts, one because he wanted the claiming to occur because she wanted him and it was something they agreed upon, and two, he didn't want to piss her off. She could wield a mean baton, and given he couldn't hurt her— because he doubted putting his woman in a headlock and giving her a noogie would go over well—he wouldn't stand a chance if she got mad. Patricia was one tough lady!

Going over the facts didn't explain her current temper. The simmering silence at his back prickled him between the shoulders, and he debated holding his tongue, but he could almost hear his brother's goading "chicken!" Needing to know what he'd done to earn her displeasure, he asked in a rush, "Did I accidentally hurt you? Or do something wrong?"

He felt more than saw her stop dead behind him. He glanced over his shoulder at her. She appeared puzzled. "Why would you ask that?"

Feeling sheepish before her query, he shrugged. "Because you seem mad, which even I know shouldn't happen if I did it right. So if I did something wrong, or hurt you, then I'm sorry. Real sorry. I'm not as experienced as you might think." Hard to meet women when he spent a lot of time gaming in his room. "I'll do better next time."

"Next time?"

Uh-oh. The way she said it implied he'd had his chance and blown it. He'd screwed up even worse than he thought. *Way to go, loser.* Find the woman of his dreams and he sucked so bad at sex she wouldn't even contemplate a second round.

With his hands tethered so he couldn't smack himself, and his brothers too far away to help, he did the next best thing and banged his head off the wall.

"What the hell are you doing?"

"Punishing myself for being a dumbass," he replied in a morose voice.

"Oh for Pete's sake. You didn't do anything wrong."

"If I didn't, then why do you seem so angry? And why won't you let me try again? I promise to do better." Someone kill him now. He'd gone from bad lover to pathetic whiner. He banged his head again.

"Would you stop that!" She grabbed him and prevented him from giving himself the concussion he deserved. His brothers had no problems seducing their mates and getting them to smile after sex. Why couldn't he have inherited the same skill? "I'm not mad at you, but myself."

"Why? You were perfect." Divine. Heavenly. He could have waxed eloquent on her attributes, but he didn't want to come across as too needy or nerdy —which she probably already suspected he was. No one should ever admit they used to read a thesaurus when they went to the john.

"I'm mad because I didn't mean for that to happen or for things to progress as they did."

"You didn't want to have sex with me?" Way to soothe his ego. Not! He went to smack himself again, but she put a hand in between his head and the wall before he could hit the concrete.

"Actually I did. Which is problem number one. I've wanted to tear off your clothes since we met. But I shouldn't. It's wrong. So damned wrong."

In a rare moment of insight, Stu verbalized the reason, "Because you feel like you're being disloyal to your previous mate."

"Bingo." She released a tired breath. "You're an attractive guy, Stu. Even though I have a list of reasons why I shouldn't want you, my mate Ryker and your age prime among them, there's also the fact we're on a job. And I don't even want to get on the topic of the fact your roommate, Ricky, thinks I belong to him too. Then add to the whole mess, I don't even know if I'm ready to commit. The fact that I don't feel in control." An exasperated sound whooshed from her. "I mean there are all these reasons and excuses for me to stay far away from you. Heck, I was even debating ditching the whole mission and taking off for the wilds of the Rockies, I'm so damned confused."

"But you didn't."

"No. I didn't. I couldn't. I'm not a coward, and I take my responsibilities seriously. Usually nothing manages to distract me from my tasks. But you …" She waved a hand in his direction. "Ricky. Everything. I just don't know if I can handle all this right now."

A part of him marveled at her frankness, and a part of him feared saying the wrong thing and having her clam up, but he couldn't resist asking, "If you're so determined to keep me away, then why did you seduce me?"

A sharp sound came from her, a cross between a laugh and a disparaging snort. "Because you were too damned tempting."

"Me?" He practically choked on the word. In his lifetime, many words described him. Geeky. Slob. Pest. Gaming god. Five-finger specialist. But tempting? Usually that was a word used to describe fresh-baked cookies or the dude who modeled for that name brand underwear.

"Yes, you. I came across you looking so intent

on whatever techy thing you were doing with your computer, hair all mussed up, attention so focused, I couldn't freakn' resist."

Laughter burst forth from him. "You mean to say I tempted you with my nerdy nature?" Where was a camera to capture the most perfect moment of his life? No one would ever believe it. Hell, he'd just heard it and had a hard time processing it. *She thinks I'm hot!*

"Don't laugh or I'll hurt you." She said it with vehemence, but he could hear the humor underlying her tone.

Feeling a heck of a lot better, he smiled at her. "So I didn't suck at the whole, you know, sex thing?"

A grin curled her lips. She reached out a hand and brushed his cheek, a quick stroke, before yanking it back. "No. On the contrary, you were quite good."

Mental fist pump! "Really?"

"Yes really. I'd say those years of handling a game controller have paid off. When it comes to pressing buttons, you're a pro."

She said it with a grin, and Stu laughed, only to lose his smile a second later as he remembered her earlier words. "You say that, and yet you seemed quite adamant about not doing it again."

"And here we come back to the guilt factor. I enjoyed it, but hate myself for it. You don't need to tell me I'm messed up."

"No, you're just normal. It will take time for you to adjust your thinking. I can wait." Because she was worth it.

"Wait?" She snorted. "Much as I say now it won't happen again, I already feel the urge to drag you off somewhere and do wicked things to you." Oh, how his heart swelled to hear it. She must have caught his elation because she growled. "Don't look so pleased. Tempting or not, I intend to fight it. We have a job to do."

"I know, and I'll do my best to not drive you wild with lust for my body."

It was her turn to laugh. "And here you are doing it again. Being too damned understanding and adorable. I totally blame you if I jump you again because I can't help myself." How aggrieved she sounded.

He'd never heard anything more beautiful. "Well, until you clear your head and decide what you want, I shall strive to keep my sexy geekiness under wraps."

A smile curved one corner of her lips. "You do that, wolf. Now come on. We've lingered long enough. I'm surprised we haven't been called out for loitering. It's almost lights out."

Turning to face the other way, they began their prisoner march, entering a zone under surveillance. Or not. "This is odd," Stu said, a frown between his brows as he stared up at the camera. No red light flashed. "The camera in this hall is dead."

Patricia peeked to where he pointed. "How can you tell?"

"This model has a blinking red light to show when they're functioning. It's an easy way to spot when maintenance is required, or if they go offline, especially in places where the cameras don't always have someone manning them."

"I wonder if this is the only one," she mused.

"Come on, let's hit your cell and find out."

With gentler hands than before, she marched him to the next set of doors and another corridor with a dead camera. It was only as they drew close to his temporary home that he thought to ask, "Why are we going back here? I thought your plan for the evening involved me going to the infirmary with a tummy ache."

"That was before it occurred to me that a woman could be the one doing the crime. Which means you wouldn't be safe there. What if the nurse is the one killing shifters? She could have you suffer an accident while in her care."

"It would bother you if I got hurt?"

"Of course it would, idiot. I might not know what I want, but I can definitely say I don't want to see you hurt."

"I'm growing on you." He couldn't help but crow it.

"Slow down, puppy. I barely know you."

"But you like me."

"A little."

A small admission, but he'd take it. He also didn't push it. As they neared his cell, his step slowed as something unpleasant occurred to him. "What should I tell Ricky?"

"Tell him I changed the plan."

"Not about that, about, you know." He lowered his voice to say in a conspiratorial whisper, "The fact we had sex."

"Oh. That." She paused. "Do we have to?"

"He's going to smell it."

"Shit. I don't have time to get us both

showered. Damn. Damn. Damn."

Stu didn't know whether he should be insulted or worried that she cared so much what Ricky thought.

He settled for smug, an expression he couldn't help but wear when he saw Ricky at the bars to their cell, wearing a glower that practically melted everything in its path.

"Well, well, well. Look at what the cat dragged back."

So much for hoping his sense of smell was on the fritz. His roommate knew, and he didn't appear happy at all. This would make for an interesting evening. Here was to hoping his nose didn't get rearranged too noticeably.

Chapter Fifteen

They couldn't hide what they'd done. Stu practically burst out of his skin he was so damned pleased with himself, while Patricia wore the expression of the guilty.

Before she could tell him, Ricky faced the wall of his cell, palms against the cement surface as Patricia let Stu into the cell. The door slammed shut, and he heard the rattle as Stu's manacles were removed. Ricky didn't turn. He couldn't without fearing he'd do or say something stupid, an increasing certainty as his anger simmered, the smell of sex invading his nostrils, both taunting and pissing him off.

She won't give me an inch, won't even let me try, but she'll fuck the pup. Unfreakn' believable.

What did the young wolf have that he didn't? Ricky was bigger, stronger, an alpha to the wolf's beta. And yet the cougar chose the wimp over him? Talk about a blow to his ego—and his heart.

"I've got to do my rounds. Stu, fill Ricky in on our new theory and why the change in plan. I'll be back in a while."

She took the coward's route, striding quickly away. No matter. Ricky intended to get the facts, just not the ones involving the case. Whirling around, he couldn't help but watch the swing of her heart-shaped ass as it swung out of sight before grabbing the wolf by the throat and slamming him against the wall.

"You nervy little bastard. You fucked my woman."

Stu didn't have the intelligence to deny it or apologize. Oh no. He made things worse. "Actually, she seduced me."

Slam. He rammed Stu against the wall, surely rattling what few brain cells he possessed. "She what?" Ricky practically roared.

"You heard me. One minute, I was minding my business doing research, and the next, she had her hands all over me, and we did it."

"You claimed her."

"Not exactly."

Ricky sniffed, letting his refined olfactory senses fill in the blanks. "She didn't let you come inside her."

"No, it was my decision to pull out."

Ricky dropped the wolf and arched a brow. "You did? Why?"

Rubbing at his throat, Stu rolled his shoulders. "Because she wasn't ready."

"Not ready? What kind of bullshit is that? She was ready enough to have sex with you."

"Sex is a physical need. She needed to release some pent-up energy. I was handy. It could have just as easily been with you."

But it wasn't. Ricky scowled. "So she finally gave in to what her body is telling her? I still don't get why you didn't claim her." Because Ricky would have. He burned for the cougar, wanted her so freakn' bad it was driving him slowly mad.

"I didn't do it because I could tell she was still working through some issues. The whole losing her mate thing still bugs her. She's dealing with a lot of guilt right now."

"Guilt? But why? The guy's been dead for a few years. She's allowed to care again." To Ricky, it seemed very black and white. Her mate was dead. They weren't. Life went on. He'd learned that at a young age. Those who wallowed in the past ended up miserable and alone. Why would she choose that path?

"A part of her knows what she's feeling is normal and all right. And it's not like she's been celibate. From what I know, she's dated since his death, but dating and fucking are a lot different than getting involved in another mating. For one thing, she's probably scared of losing someone she loves again. It probably wasn't an easy thing to come back from. Then there's the whole betrayal factor."

"Betrayal? The guy's fucking dead. He wouldn't expect her to be a nun for the rest of her life."

"Of course not. But tell that to her heart. In allowing herself to care for someone else, she feels as if she's betraying this Ryker guy. Having loved him deeply, she feels guilty that she might find happiness again."

For a young guy, Stu seemed to understand the situation better than Ricky. Because if it were up to him, he'd just claim her and show her that life with him would make her happy. But, listening to Stu, he had to wonder if his heavy-handed approach might make things worse. Much as it galled him, he asked for advice. "So how do we deal with her and her issues?"

"Since when are we a 'we'?"

A grimace creased his face. "Since it looks as if, like it or not, she wants us both."

"Are you sure she wants you?" Stu taunted and almost lost his front teeth for it. Only the fear of Patricia's wrath stayed Ricky's fist.

The last thing he needed was for her to get pissed at him and more sympathetic in regards to the wolf. If the young pup could act the part of understanding suitor, then, by damn, so could he!

"She wants me. And, make no mistake, I will have her. I might not like the fact we're going to share, but so long as it's her choice, I'll abide by it. But, trust me when I say, first sign she's tired of you, I will dispose of you myself."

"Speaking of dispose …" Stu neatly changed the subject and gave Ricky a recap of his discussion with Patricia. At the end of it all, Ricky was laughing.

"You think a woman's killing shifters off? No fucking way."

"Why not? Once drugged, it's not as if the victims could put up a fight."

"I'll agree on that point, but come on? A woman? Do you know how rare female serial killers are?"

"Rare because they don't happen often, or rare because they don't get caught?" Stu countered.

"Do you always have to argue?"

"I prefer to call it debate. I was champion of it at my school."

"Dork."

"A dork who got pussy."

There was that smug look again. Ricky

snapped. Whether Patricia liked it or not, that taunt earned the wolf a punch to the face. It didn't solve anything, but Ricky sure felt a whole lot better.

Chapter Sixteen

As it turned out, it wasn't just a few corridors with malfunctioning cameras, but all of them. A system-wide glitch had taken all the cameras offline, leaving the guards blind. A technician had been called in to repair the problem, but he seemed to think it would be hours before he could resolve the issue.

In a sense it was a blessing in disguise for Patricia. It meant less chance of her actions going noticed as she forewent the pre-planned route of her rounds to check on the shifters in her care. As if the moon goddess herself were on her side, they were short-shifted. A large number of guards called in sick, citing some kind of stomach flu that struck fast and furious.

No surveillance. A skeleton crew of guards. Patricia didn't believe in coincidences. *It's like someone is setting the scene. A scene for murder.* But, this time, their perfectly plotted plan would fail, and their luck would run out because Patricia would catch them and bring them in to the council to pay for their crimes.

Because of safety concerns, a memo went out ordering the few guards who did show up to abstain from performing their usual rounds out of fear something would happen without anyone seeing and being able to come to their aid. The news was met with cheers. The evening staff split off to man certain key points in the prison. Behind their locked doors, they pulled out cards and cellphones and hunkered down for an evening of game play and social networking.

Patricia, however, didn't have time to check out the latest YouTube video or pass level one hundred and forty-seven in Candy Crush—which was impossible. The knot in her gut said the killer would strike tonight. The question, though, was, who would the killer target?

Slipping away from her assigned guard post proved easy. New to the job, she'd not yet made an impression on those she worked with. She told the guy she was paired with she had orders to report to another location, and engrossed in his sexting with his girlfriend, he barely noticed when she left. She also doubted he'd double check to see if she made it safely.

Master key ring in her possession, courtesy of the shifter council who'd had a duplicate set created to aid her in her task, she made her way back to Ricky and Stu's cell to check on them. She convinced herself that her first priority was to inform them of the state of the cameras and, at the same time, verify their safety.

What a load of bull. Stu already knew something was wonky with the surveillance system, which meant Ricky knew. As for their wellbeing, even she couldn't deny that, as a pair, they stood the best chance of surviving an attack. So why did she choose them over the other possible victims? The real reason?

I'm worried about them.

The hairy truth almost gagged her. What if the killer went after them? What if Patricia wasn't there to protect them? Stupid and irrational considering the guys were capable of looking after themselves, especially since they knew to watch for anything suspicious. Heck, she could practically picture Ricky scoffing at her instinct to guard. Even alone, that rough cat would land on his feet and probably not even lose one of his nine lives in the process.

What about Stu though? While a big guy, he possessed a bit of a naïve spirit when it came to women. Would he have what it took to take a female killer down? He seemed the type to hesitate out of misplaced chivalry, making him a prime target. She couldn't let that happen. *I need to protect him from his darned gentlemanly morals.*

That was if her theory about the killer being a woman panned out. The more she mulled it though, the more and more it made the most sense. Even before she brought Stu on board, she and the shifters' council operatives had run through the personnel files of those employed at the prisons and done facial comparisons on employee rosters for the men. But one only had to see the ever-increasing death toll to realize someone kept eluding them. Who better than a benign woman whose stature or appearance would have those looking give her a pass because they'd assume 'no way'?

Having been underestimated too many times to count in her career, Patricia wasn't so quick to dismiss, hence why she justified her hurried pace to the cell of her undercover partners.

Good idea. Find our mates, purred her cougar. *Mark them and keep them close.* More and more, her cat refused to stay silent, making her wishes known, if not quite verbally, then through emotion. And, tonight of all nights, with the moon pulling at her wilder side, the animal instinct she hid most of the time threatened to surface. What would happen if she lost hold of the leash she kept on her inner beast?

I'd probably wake up in the morning naked, fucked, and bitten. A mating marriage under a full moon that would bind her to one or more men for life. Would that truly be so bad?

Yes! No. Maybe.

A frustrated snarl passed her lips. While a part of Patricia continued to defy this uncontrollable urge, a larger part, which grew day by day, hour by hour, wanted to give in. In a sense she already had when she seduced Stu.

Sweet Stu. Awkward and geeky on the outside, but an ardent lover and more understanding man than she would have given credit. Facing him again filled her stomach with girlish butterflies.

Then there was Ricky. Hot, domineering, and determined. Everything she avoided in a man.

If only I could somehow avoid him altogether. Because she feared, despite her guilt over betraying Ryker's memory, she wouldn't be able to resist the next time Ricky cornered her.

A smart girl, intent on remaining single and true to her memories, would keep herself far away from the temptation they posed. Apparently, she wasn't as smart as she liked to believe.

I should stay away. Face them later.

Coward. It wasn't just guilt and fear over what she might do that made her question her choice to go see her partners. A part of her didn't want to deal with the anger Ricky was sure to exude as he confronted her over her choice to seduce Stu, an anger she'd seen simmering before and run from, leaving Stu to face it alone.

Oops. Too late, it occurred to her that by taking the coward's route she'd left Stu in a difficult spot. A possibly dangerous one. Ricky made no pretense about his jealousy. Would he act on it?

He better not have hurt Stu. And if he had? What would she do? Punish Ricky? Hadn't she already by not giving in to his overtures? By choosing the young wolf over him?

Why couldn't she rewind the clock to a time before she'd met them? A time when all she worried about was who Emily Thorne would target next on *Revenge*?

Patricia didn't need to announce her presence, not when whispers and catcalls followed her rapid steps along the dark corridor. Despite the late hour, not all the prisoners slept, and many tracked her progress with sly comments and invitations to make a prostitute blush.

She ignored them all. The knot in her gut urged her to hurry. Something was amiss. She didn't realize she held her breath until she saw Ricky and Stu at the bars to their cell.

"What is it, *bebé*? You appear anxious."

To her relief, Ricky met her with concern, not accusation. "I was worried about you." The admission slipped out before she could stop it.

A soft chuckle rumbled, teasing along her skin, making it prickle. "We're fine for the moment. But my cat's restless."

"My wolf is giving me a headache with his

whining," Stu grumbled. "I don't know if it's the full moon or something else, but he is really pushing to get out."

So she wasn't alone in sensing something amiss. "I think something's about to happen. I need to check on the other two prisoners."

"Alone?"

With her enhanced eyesight, she had no problem seeing the frown on Ricky's face, and Stu seemed none too pleased either. "It's not like I can ask the other guards for help."

"It's not safe."

"It's my job."

"Then take us with you."

Her first impulse was to say no. She worked alone, but Stu added his two cents before she could voice a word.

"He's right. There's something not right about the whole camera thing."

"Obviously, which is why I need to get to the others to check on them before something happens."

"Not alone. It's too dangerous." Ricky stuck to his stubborn he-man claim.

"Have you forgotten what I do for a living? I'm trained to take down criminals."

"Humans, usually, with a gun. What do you have right now? A baton? What if the perp is a shifter like us? Or is armed? How will you handle it alone?"

Ricky made valid points, but what else did he expect her to do, sit around twiddling her thumbs? The whole purpose of their mission was for them to catch the culprit. She'd hoped they could do it via investigative work that would have led them to the perp outside of jail, where a squad of shifters could help out. Alas, they still didn't have a clue, but if she could catch the murderer red-handed, she could end this tonight. "I am not going to hide and let the killer strike."

"Then take me with you," Ricky boldly said.

"I can't take you with me," she sputtered. "You're prisoners. If anyone sees me with you, you'll blow your cover."

"Better we blow our cover than send you off alone to possibly confront a killer."

"I'll be fine. Whoever it is hasn't attacked guards before. Just inmates." She was bluffing. She had no idea if any guards had died. They'd only really researched inmate deaths. It never occurred to them to look beyond the walls of the prison.

Apparently, Ricky had put more thought into this than she had. "The killer is going after shifters. We don't know that they'll make a distinction between guard and prisoner. I, for one, don't want to take that chance. Open this door and take me with you."

For some reason, his acute observation about the possibility of the killer going after any shifter, inmate or not, pissed her off. *Who's the cop here?* "No."

"Don't push me on this, *bebé*." Ricky's eyes flashed yellow as his temper flared to the surface.

"Are you giving me an ultimatum?" She pursed her lips and crossed her arms over her chest. She didn't take well to orders. Even well-meaning ones.

"Yes. I am."

She laughed. "And how do you plan on enforcing it? In case you hadn't noticed, you're behind bars. What's to stop me from walking away?"

"Are you that determined and stubborn to spite me that you would prefer to put yourself in harm's way than accept my help?"

Yes! Even she saw how illogical that was. But she suspected an ulterior motive. "You want more than just to help me."

"True. I won't lie. I mean to claim you. Just like the wolf here intends to place his mark when you allow him to."

"When she's ready," Stu interjected, having acted as a silent observer to their argument 'til this point.

At least the wolf had the common sense not to push her buttons. Stu understood her. "Will you wait until I am ready as well?" She arched a brow in query.

"No." A sensual smile stretched Ricky's lips, and his eyes practically glowed as he caught her gaze. The more they stood staring at each other, caught in a face off, the more golden they turned. Dizzying. Full of promises. And delights ... She blinked first. Ricky grinned in triumph. "Unlike my young friend, I am not a man who waits on the whimsy of others. I see what I want, and I take it. And I definitely want you."

She couldn't help how her skin prickled, especially when he raked a smoldering gaze over her body that left no part of her untouched. He threw down the gauntlet, and she should have exploded into a fury. Instead, heat flooded her body as a part of her, a submissive girly part she would have claimed didn't exist—and immediately wanted to slap silly—exploded with pleasure and ached for him to act on his words. She squashed it as best she could, but feared he'd caught the rise in her body's temperature by the knowing half smirk on his lips. "Take it? I thought you'd turned over a new leaf? No more stealing and taking things that don't belong to you."

"It is not theft to take what is rightfully mine."

"I'm not yours."

"Yet."

Curse the flood of moisture his words brought. "You're an arrogant prick."

"I agree. Now let me out of here. Time is wasting while we discuss the inevitable."

"And how am I supposed to explain wandering around the prison with a pair of prisoners?"

"You won't have to, but they might want to know how the dangerous panther and wolf got in."

She blinked, sure she'd misunderstood. "Excuse me, but I thought I heard you say you want to go as your animals?"

"I did. We'll track better if we do."

"What of the prisoners? Not all of them are sleeping," she hissed, having a hard time keeping her voice down. Instinct said the occupants in the cells nearest to them slumbered, but who knew who listened? And what they'd say.

"Who is going to believe them when they

claim they saw a wolf, a panther, and a cougar roaming the halls."

"I can't go as my cat."

"Why not?"

"Locked doors in our path, or have you forgotten where we are?" she snapped.

"Good point. You stay dressed and take care of any locks. I'll take point while Stu guards our rear."

"You have this all planned out."

His cocky grin should have merited a slap, but almost got a kiss. It was crazy how much he appealed with his macho demands and domineering treatment. Used to fighting male chauvinism on a daily basis, a part of her couldn't understand why it turned her on. Was it the fact she had to act so tough all the time that made her crave it? She'd have to analyze that later. They'd spent too much time arguing. If he wanted to blow their cover, then so be it. At least if he got removed then she wouldn't have to face him every day, and then maybe she could go back to her sterile—lonely—existence.

Ha. As if that would happen. The cat—known as lust and need—was out of the bag, and it was going to get some satisfaction. Whether Patricia liked it or not.

Chapter Seventeen

"You'd better behave," she admonished as she sorted through her jangling set of keys.

Like that would happen. Ricky couldn't believe his arguing had worked. Despite her evident desire not to, Patricia set them loose. But the click and clanking as she opened their cell brought attention to them. Even though the other prisoners couldn't see in the dark, it didn't prevent them from calling out.

"Someone's getting lucky," a voice sang out.

"Come on over here and set me free. I'll pay you. I've got money."

A face pressed against the bars right across from them. The beady-eyed prisoner smacked his lips and uttered a disgusting, "Lucky bastard. What I wouldn't give to tap that fine, fucking ass."

It took Ricky only two long strides to reach the speaker. Reaching through the bars, he grabbed a hold of the guy with the foul mouth and slammed his face against them, once, twice. The now silent prisoner slid to the floor.

"Was that really necessary?" Patricia hissed.

"Yes. I didn't want him kicking up a fuss and alerting any of the guards." Not the entire truth. No one spoke of his woman like that in his hearing. To his surprise, the wolf backed him up.

"If he hadn't done it, I would have. That's no way to talk to a lady."

Her jaw dropped at Stu's words, and Ricky

couldn't help but smile as he used a finger to push it shut. "Save that look for later when I show you something truly amazing. Let's go find ourselves a killer."

Stripping out of their prison wear, it took only moments to shift into their beasts, the dark color of their fur blending in better with the shadows than their prison oranges would have.

Mumbling under her breath about "Moon madness makes me do the stupidest things," Patricia took off at a brisk walk.

Despite the sweet view of her ass as she strutted, Ricky slipped by her to take the lead, all his senses on alert for danger or anything out of the ordinary. As he slunk along, belly low to the floor, he couldn't help but ponder his situation. More accurately, Patricia.

When Ricky was first confronted by the fact she'd seduced Stu, his initial anger had contained an element of hurt. Why choose the weaker wolf over him? Did she prefer a submissive male? Because, no matter the attraction or what his feline thought, Ricky wouldn't roll over and bare his belly for anyone, not even his mate. Nor would he pretend to, not even to claim her. A man had his pride. *I earned my man card fair and square, and no cougar, no matter how hot, is going to make me give it up.*

Despite the risk of antagonizing her, he stuck true to himself, telling her outright that he would claim her. He didn't hide his domineering traits because that was who he was, take it or leave it.

Her arousal spiked, and an interesting thing became clear. Despite her attraction to Stu and his beta nature, she was also drawn to Ricky, especially when he attempted to dominate her.

No matter what she says, she likes it when I give her orders. Her very scent gave it away. Perhaps fate wasn't so crazy when it had chosen two men for the cougar. On the one hand, she craved power over a male, probably because of her day-to-day job. Stu, with his beta nature, would fit the bill or at least satisfy that craving. However, another part of her, a part she kept hidden from the world, needed a man to take charge, to pull the reins of control from her capable hands and remind her that she could rely on someone other than herself. *And that man is me. I will remind her she is a woman and that she doesn't always have to be the one making decisions.*

Seen in this light, it all made perfect sense. But would she accept it or continue to fight?

Given her seduction of Stu, and her capitulation to Ricky's demands, he sensed she approached the tipping point. It wouldn't take much to have her fall into his arms—and onto his dick. The question was, would he take advantage and mark her or, like the wolf had, grant her some leeway to accept her fate and agree to the mating on her own?

A decision he'd have to make later, or in the heat of the moment, because Patricia broke his train of thought with a whispered, "Kirkland's cell is just up ahead. He's a wolf like Stu. Quiet sort. In for drug trafficking, nothing violent. He shares his space with a human." She paused to sniff the air. "I don't smell anything out of the ordinary. What about you guys?"

Ricky shook his head, as did Stu, their animal shape preventing speech. Despite the lack of scent,

Ricky pricked his ears, searching for any sounds out of the ordinary … but nothing jumped out.

This wing of the prison was fairly silent with only the rumbles and snorts of sleeping people to break the stillness. As a matter of fact, they were the noisiest things around. Their footsteps, the occasion scuff of her shoe, the soft pad of their furry feet screamed to him, but apparently weren't loud enough to be heard over the steady snoring of the cell occupants, one of whom was the shifter they sought.

Patricia came to a halt before the bars, but there was nothing to see, attack, or do. Curled in a fetal position on his bunk, the wolf didn't even twitch, despite the fact two predators stood outside the cell.

Then again, given he'd lived here almost three years, his senses had probably dulled. Ricky vowed to never let himself get that complacent. There was something unnerving about sneaking up on another shifter so easily. He would never want anyone to catch him so vulnerable.

Stu shifted to his man shape, man parts dangling. It irritated Ricky to see he had competition in that department. *So much for wowing her with my bigger dick.*

Unheeding of his nakedness, Stu left them to check something out on the ceiling.

"What are you doing?" Patricia asked, echoing the question Ricky couldn't utter while in his cat form.

"Checking for tampering with the camera. It's dead like the others, but I see no sign of extra sabotage. No paint across the lens. No obstruction."

He grabbed the door separating this section from the next and gave it a tug. It didn't move. "Door is still locked."

"The other prisons didn't show signs of damage to the cameras."

"They also didn't mention any outages, but in retrospect, I now have to wonder how many of them went down during the time frames in question."

"Not all the prisons have surveillance systems of the cells in place. Some only have cameras in the common areas."

"You said there was a technician working on the problem? Did he mention if it was a hardware or software problem?"

Patricia shrugged. "I don't know, and I didn't ask. Management told us they were down and probably would be for hours. That's it."

"Given the killer can't be sure when the cameras will come back on line, and the fact we're not seeing any signs of tampering, I'd say this guy is as safe as can be at the moment."

"You really think so?"

"Not really. I just know that if I was the one planning anything, cameras down or not, I'd be putting some paint or tape across the lenses at the very least, just in case. Then again, it's possible the attacker just hasn't made it to this section yet. For all I know, the killer will strike as soon as we leave. Short of having someone on watch, we won't really know. " Stu lifted his shoulders in a helpless gesture.

"What are you suggesting? That I leave one of you behind to keep an eye?"

Ricky growled to show his disapproval. There

was safety in numbers, especially given they didn't know who or what they faced. Thankfully, Patricia agreed, else he might have had to butt heads with her again, the stubborn one, not the horny one.

"The killer doesn't usually go after those with a roommate. I'd say this guy is safe for the moment. We should move on to the next one. He's down in solitary."

"How come? I thought he was a quiet guy," Stu asked.

"He is. But someone touched his pudding today at lunch. Apparently, he really likes his pudding."

Liked it enough that he snapped and smashed the offender's face off a table enough times to break his two front teeth. Ricky had heard about the lunch time entertainment through the grapevine.

"Then I guess we're visiting the solitary wing."

"Or not. Problem is I don't know how we'll get past the guards. For some reason, despite being short-handed, management insisted we post a pair there."

"Leave that to me," Stu muttered. "I used to run interference for my brothers all the time so they could sneak out and meet with girls."

Just how many brothers did Stu have? He'd alluded before to coming from a large family, but Ricky never really questioned him about it. He'd never actually cared. However, if they were going to end up partners in some kind of weird ménage triangle, he'd probably have to find out. Just so he could know what he faced in case Stu's brothers took offense that their brother had to share his woman.

"Exactly what are you planning?"

"Better I don't tell you, you'll just tell me no." Stu grinned. "Oh, and you don't happen to have any tape, do you?"

"I brought some duct tape with me in case I needed to silence someone. Why do you ask?"

"Do me a favor and don't lock any of the doors we go through next. Actually, unlock anything that isn't a cell and tape the latch so it just takes a nudge to swing it open. If this is going to work, I need unobstructed passage."

"Won't leaving the path open make it easier for our killer?"

"Seeing as how it's never proven a problem before, does it matter?"

"Still, as a member of law enforcement, I have to say this makes me uncomfortable. You do know this a prison, right? Filled with bad guys? Isn't making it unsecure kind of dangerous?"

"Do you have a better plan then?"

"Unlocked doors might tip them off that something's wrong and scare them off."

"And save lives, which is still our primary objective."

"You take arguing to a whole new level."

"It's my speciality. Now, can we just concede and get on with it?"

"This better work," she grumbled as she unlocked the door and taped the latch. They then retraced their steps, thankfully not far, to create a clear path back to their cell in case they needed to get back in a hurry.

Escape route taken care of, once again they took off in their silent train, Ricky in the lead, Patricia close behind, and Stu following at the rear, once again in his wolf shape. The deeper they went, the more the silence pressed in on them. The air itself grew heavy, oppressive even. Ricky could almost taste the wrongness.

Whatever they searched for, it was close. If Ricky's instinct could be trusted, they needed to get beyond the circle of light signaling the checkpoint before the solitary cells. Just one snag. A pair of guards sat at a battered metal desk bolted to the floor, playing cards.

They retreated. Time for a powwow.

Patricia led them back to a storage closet she'd unlocked on their way toward the solitary wing. Once inside, Ricky was about to shift, only to realize Stu hadn't followed. Ducking his head out to see where the wolf had gotten to, he noted him back up the hall, just outside the lit antechamber.

"Where's Stu?" Patricia hissed from behind him.

About to take care of their guard situation, something she realized only a second after posing her question.

"Idiot," she muttered. She kicked off her shoes to make less noise before she bolted up the hall after him. He would guess she intended to yank Stu to safety, but that wouldn't help them with their need to get past the guards. Like it or not, they needed a diversion, and the wolf, recognizing this, had volunteered.

The guy had more guts than Ricky initially

gave him credit for. *He's not so bad for a dumb mutt.* If his feline could have smiled, it would have. Instead, Ricky padded after Patricia. Before either of them could catch the wolf, he trotted boldly out into the light.

When Patricia would have followed, Ricky head-butted her. Catching his hint, she held back, the pair of them hiding in the shadows watching the unfolding events, close enough to jump in and help if needed.

Human Stu bore a shaggy appearance and his wolf proved just as scruffy with his hair sticking out wildly in all directions, the colors varying shades of brown. As if wild animals of his ilk did it every day, Stu approached the card-playing guards, and when they didn't immediately notice his presence— probably because they'd been imbibing from a flask that dulled their senses—he circled around to the other side of the desk and yipped.

Well, that got him some attention. Two sets of eyes whirled his way. Widened. Mouths dropped open, and one uttered a, "Holy shit."

They couldn't scramble from their seats fast enough, not to chase Stu, who wagged his tail, but to run in the opposite direction, right toward Patricia and Ricky.

Good thing they had good reflexes and speed. They slid into the storage closet and shut the door without a second to spare as the guards came bolting down the hall, Stu at their heels. Only once they passed did she curse aloud. "Damn it. What is he thinking? I thought the plan was to stick together. Not go haring off."

Swapping his cat for his male shape, Ricky tried to soothe her. "He'll be fine. That wolf is wilier than I initially gave him credit for."

"Wily but naïve. And he's all alone. God only knows who he could run into. Like a killer."

"You worry too much, *bebé*."

"Someone has to."

Even in the dark of the closet, he could see the lines of stress on her forehead. He couldn't resist stepping forward and placing a kiss upon them in an attempt to smooth them out. "He'll be fine."

She opened her mouth to retort, but he swallowed any further protest by placing his lips upon hers.

Mmm, the memory of the electricity between them never came close to the reality. How sweet she tasted. Her lips opened at his touch, unfurling and softening, a flower burgeoning before the heat of his caress.

This is the wrong place and time, his conscience tried to tell him.

Screw their mission or reason for being here. He needed this. Needed Patricia. He'd felt so denied these past few days, a stranger in his own skin, with wants and desires that consumed him and overshadowed his every waking thought and fantasy.

His hands gripped her buttocks, the coarse linen of her slacks not hiding their round fullness. He pulled her against him, pressing his aching cock against her lower belly, the rough fabric of her clothing chafing his skin. What he wouldn't give to feel her silky body against his. He dragged his embrace from the sweetness of her lips to the smoothness of her neck, sucking and licking at the flesh, working his way lower and lower.

She gasped his name, a sweet entreaty. "Ricky."

"Shh. Just relax and let me ease your tension." He continued to caress her, the perfume of her arousal heady in the closed space.

"We shouldn't. We need to check on the prisoner."

How insulting that she thought of work at a time like this. Lust should consume her just as it consumed him. How could she manage coherent thought when he could barely remember his own name?

"Are you sure he can't wait a few more minutes?" He pushed the palm of his hand against her still- covered pussy, the heat of her core radiating forth. How he wanted a lick.

She moaned. "Why must you make this so hard?"

"This is hard." He grabbed her hand and placed it upon his swollen cock.

Her fingers closed around him, and it was his turn to suck in a ragged breath.

"That's it, *bebé*. Stroke me. Touch me. See how much I desire you. Need you. You can't tell me you don't feel the same thing too."

For a moment, he thought she'd once again deny what flowered between them. She surprised him. "I shouldn't want you," she admitted, her voice low and guilt-ridden. "God knows I keep fighting it. Telling myself I'm better off walking away."

"But …"

A sigh fluttered across his lips as he faced her, his forehead touching hers in the ultimate intimacy and sharing of space.

"I can't help myself it seems. No matter how wrong I tell myself this is or how many times I try to tell myself you're not my type, that I need to focus, I can't help but want you."

Her admission swelled his heart, made his inner feline purr and, despite his hunger for her, allowed him to do the right thing—for her at any rate. "I guess I'll have to accept that for now. I don't want you distracted the first time we come together. Come on. Let's go check on our shifter before Stu tires of chasing the guards and they come back."

What no sex? His panther screamed in protest, an echoing cry that, despite being only in his mind, almost made him wince. But Ricky knew he'd made the right choice. Yes, he could have made her melt. Yes, he could have taken her, quickly too, but did he want her resenting their first time?

He did the right—if painful—thing.

Ricky clasped her hand in his, a twining of fingers that initially she stiffened at. He squeezed and she relaxed enough to curl them around his. Hand in hand, they inched from their hiding spot and crept up the hall. While he kept watch, she fitted the key to open the door, keeping the solitary wing confined, and after securing the latch with tape, they sneaked in.

Here there wasn't the same kind of silence they'd encountered in other parts of the prison. A lone voice sang, kind of. The disjointed notes and nonsense words were nothing Ricky recognized, but the scent was clear. Whoever belted out the off-key symphony was their shifter, alive and well.

"I guess that answers that question," Ricky said, halting before the door hiding the crazy bear.

"I don't get it." Patricia frowned. "I thought for sure the killer would strike. Hell, my gut still says something's wrong. We're missing something."

"Perhaps we're too early?"

"Or we spooked them off."

"Are there any other ways into this section?"

"The door at the end, but because it leads to a hall with access to the outdoors, it has a built-in alarm that automatically trips every time it's opened."

"Any way of telling if it's been disabled?"

She shrugged. "Not unless we set it off."

"So what should we do?"

"I don't know." She gnawed her lower lip and turned in a circle, checking their location out. "If only there was a place nearby for us to hide."

"The closet?"

"Too far. What if the killer did manage to disable the alarm and came through the far end? We'd never see or hear them."

"We could hide in an empty cell."

"I guess." Her response emerged slowly and reluctantly. Oh ho, did the thought of being alone with him in a small space, with only a cot as furniture, bother her?

Excellent.

"What are you waiting for? Let's hide."

"What about, Stu?"

"There's nothing we can do for the wolf. You'll have to trust him. Now stop arguing and let's get into our spot. We wouldn't want to spook our killer."

Even as she let them into the empty cell across from the singing bear, she continued to argue. "What if we're wrong and the perp goes after the other guy?"

"Do you really think we should split up?"

"No. Yes. I don't know. I really wish they'd given me more resources," she grumbled as she yanked the duct tape from her pocket and taped the lock so it wouldn't catch. She pushed the door shut before she slumped to the floor beside it. "They made it sound so easy when they assigned me this job," she admitted in a low whisper. "Go undercover. Keep my eyes and ears open. Provide support to the recruits posing as prisoners. Catch the killer."

"So far you've achieved the first few. We just need to catch ourselves a bad guy, or girl," he amended, "and mission accomplished."

"Yeah, if we're in the right place. At the right time. What if I chose wrong? What if they go after the other guy? Or Stu? For all we know, he went back to his cell, and he could end up a target. He's a civilian. He should be top of my priority list." She went to rise, but he stayed her with a hand.

"Stu's a big boy. He can handle himself. And, besides, the killer doesn't know Stu's alone in the cell. Not to mention our wolf won't be sleeping I'll bet. No way will anyone sneak up on him. You've got to stop stressing. You can't be in three places at once. Logic says, the guy in solitary is the most likely target, so he's the one we'll watch."

"And if we're wrong?"

"Then be mad at the killer not yourself. Better yet, blame the council for not giving you more help."

"Easy for you to say."

"No, it's not. I don't like to see anyone made a victim."

"Says the guy with a criminal past."

"A past he now regrets. I'm not proud of the things I did, but I learned from them. I also speak from experience when I say some evils can't be stopped. You can only try your best."

"I've been meaning to ask, why are you here? Why do this?"

"If you've read my file, then you know about my brother."

"Yeah, I read about him. But, I'll be honest, you seem more like the type to hunt down the person who did you wrong and take care of it yourself than volunteer to work within a set of rules and boundaries such as the ones the council probably placed on this mission."

"I'll admit a part of me just wants to tear the person who killed my brother into tiny pieces." *Rip them bloody and eat our enemy,* his cat agreed. Blood-thirsty savage.

"I sense a 'but'."

"But part of my redemption, my new way of living, means obeying society's laws. Doing things by the book. If I let myself take the easy path, even if it feels good or I can justify it, that doesn't make it the right one. The slope to depravity is slippery. It's always waiting to catch the unwary. I slid down that hillside once before and had to fight like a bastard to get back up. No matter how much I want vengeance,

I can't allow myself to give in to my violent side."

"And yet you had no problem smashing that guy's face against the bars for insulting me. Or kicking that thug's ass in the prison yard."

"I didn't say I was perfect. But, to answer your question, chivalry is allowed. In both those cases, I was coming to someone's defense." He winked.

She shook her head, sending her short blonde bob swinging. "You know, for a guy who looks like he belongs in a biker gang, you've got surprising depth."

"Shh. Don't tell anyone. I'd hate for word to get back to the juvies I work with. My badass rep is what helps keep them in line and listening to what I have to say." He grinned, and his heart skipped a beat when an answering one stretched her lips.

It occurred to him the oddity of their situation in that moment. Here he crouched, naked in front of the woman he wanted as mate, and he'd managed for several minutes to not only control his lust but also have a real conversation. Of course, as soon as he realized that, his cock swelled, he became aware of their seclusion, and being a man not to look opportunity in the eye, he leaned in for a kiss.

Chapter Eighteen

Full moons always heralded some kind of strangeness. Crime rates increased. Women went into labor early. Folks did crazy stuff.

And cougars with strong work ethics, on a life or death mission, succumbed to passion in a jail cell of all places.

In her defense, he started it!

First by opening up and speaking to her so frankly. Giving her the mental support she so needed as frustration and fear of failure threatened to drag her down. He showed her a side of him she could respect, admire, and desire. When he kissed her, it just lit the match to the tinder already waiting to catch fire.

Blame it on the lunar madness or her emotional turmoil or even the damned mating bond she'd fought since meeting. All valid excuses. All bullshit. The simple truth was she wanted him to kiss her. To touch her. To lay her upon the simple cot and cover her body with his.

This is so wrong, whispered one part of her. *This is so right,* whispered her other half.

"Relax," Ricky whispered in her ear before tugging at the lobe with his teeth.

"How will we hear if we're making out?" she muttered as his hands busied themselves tugging her button down shirt from her pants.

"Don't worry. My panther is keeping watch for us. He won't let anyone sneak up."

Her cougar purred, approving of his plan. Horny pussy. It occurred to her to protest. How dare Ricky once again think to dictate what they do? She opened her mouth to argue, but her body betrayed her, arching at his touch and sizzling with heat.

"I won't let you claim me," she said, then gasped as Ricky hiked her shirt high enough to cup her breasts, his thumbs brushing over the lace-clad peaks. The thin material enhanced the sensation, and the heat in her sex turned into a pulse. He rolled her erect nipples, and the pulse beat faster and wiped all reason from her mind.

Further argument seemed pointless, not with her body begging for more. Ricky's mouth plastered to hers. As he embraced her with a fierce passion, she forgot everything except the building pleasure in her body. When he dragged his lips from hers, she mewled in loss, but he wasn't done. He trailed blazing kisses along her jawline to her ear. A swirl of his tongue inside the delicate shell sent shivers running down her spine as he located her sensitive spots and took full advantage of them.

His mouth wasn't the only busy thing. His hands roamed her body and teased her skin. Locating the clasp to her bra, he undid it, freeing her breasts for his touch. Oh, and touch them he did, cupping them, teasing the nipples with light circling strokes of his thumb until they pointed into aching peaks. She almost begged at that point for him to do something. Thankfully, she didn't have to, as his mouth closed first over one erect nub then the other, sucking and tongue swirling, each stroke, each sensation, sending a jolt of pure desire to her wet pussy.

When she cried out, he shushed her, placing his mouth upon hers, his tongue performing a sensuous dance along hers. His lower body pressed against her thighs, and she spread them as wide as she could on the slender cot to accommodate him. The naked heat of his body burned her still-clothed bottom half. The hardness of his cock pulsed against her. She ached to feel his firm flesh within her. Fucking her.

He rubbed against her, and despite the fact his mouth clung to hers, he purred, a rumbling vibration that caused her to shudder. She couldn't help but purr back in response. The moment was too perfect, too erotic for her not to express enjoyment.

Cream pooled in her sex as her arousal coiled, ready to spring. She struggled not to make a sound but couldn't help the panting as she clung to his broad shoulders, digging her fingers into the hard muscle.

Once again, his mouth left hers, but this time, she bit her tongue even before he shushed her. Quiet. They needed to be quiet. She couldn't remember why but knew it was necessary.

Ricky slid down her body, his hands tugging at her pants, which had somehow come undone. Once he'd bared her and tossed her pants to the side, he peered at her, his eyes a smoldering gold inferno.

"So fucking beautiful," he growled. "And mine."

His dominant claim almost managed to get her hackles up, but before she could decry his possessive statement, he bent his head and settled it between her thighs. She shuddered instead, anticipation stealing her voice.

She tensed in expectation of his first lick. As if he'd give her what she wanted so easily. Oh no. He just had to show her who was in control. He teased her, rubbing the smooth edge of his jaw along the soft skin of her inner thigh. He blew warmly against her pussy, hot puffs of air that had her arching and clawing at the cot as her sex convulsed in pleasure. His tongue swiped back and forth across her pussy, lapping at her cream and stabbing between her lips. She fought not to cry out but couldn't hold in her panting breath. Need built in her, a teetering tower of passion, which he built upon; brick by pleasurable brick. When her orgasm hit, her body bowed, a taut arc with every muscle locked. And still he continued to lick. To tease her nub. To torture until she couldn't help but beg. "Fuck me."

"Will you accept me as your mate?" was his maddening reply.

She almost said yes. Almost let the needs of her body dictate the course of her future.

Sanity, a thin thread of it, prevailed, and she held back from saying the words that would bind her to this man, this maddening, glorious male, for a lifetime. He might have argued. Might have worn down her resistance and gotten his way were it not for the subtle click of a door tumbler being turned.

Chapter Nineteen

Of all the times for a killer to interrupt!

Ricky almost roared his frustration as he tore himself from the velvety sweetness of his woman to crouch by the unlatched cell door, ears pricked and listening. Arousal still coursed through his body. However, the longer he sat poised, trying to discern what happened across the hall, the more his raging hard-on diminished. But he couldn't escape the decadent aroma of Patricia's pleasure wafting in the air, flavoring his tongue and lips.

I was so close to making her mine. She might have said no for the moment, but given a few more minutes, and he would have had her purring another tune. Now the opportunity was lost, and who knew when he'd get another chance?

First, he'd have to capture the killer, probably file a damnable report, then stalk his cougar—because knowing her, she'd fight until the very end—and seduce her. He'd tie her to a bed if she proved too stubborn, and this time, he wouldn't stop until she screamed yes—preferably while his cock was buried inside her and her nails raked his back.

Despite the clear sound of a door opening, there was no murmur of voices. Peering over his shoulder at Patricia, who hastily righted her clothes and hid her delightful curves, he inclined his head with an unspoken gesture of "Do we go in?"

She nodded as she palmed her baton. He held up one finger, two … On the third, he flung open the door and charged through, heading for the gaping portal across from him. He landed in a crouch, head swinging, searching for the intruder.

Clad in black from head to toe, the shifter menace was already at work. Ricky startled the culprit as they straightened from the cot, the glinting tip of a needle projecting from the hand that had administered a drug to the sleeping shifter. It seemed the bear had gone from singing to sleeping while Ricky made love to his woman.

The killer heard him enter and whirled. Despite the ski mask hiding the majority of the features, there was no denying it. *Patricia and Stu were right.* The murderer was a woman, a petite one too, but the sneer on her delicate pinks lips was anything but gentle. Despite her humanity, she also managed a snarl worthy of a predator.

"Filthy creature," she screamed. Despite her obvious disadvantage, she lunged at him, and while he avoided the pointy end of the syringe in her hand, he couldn't miss the jab of the other she pulled from her jumpsuit. It dug into the meat of the arm he threw up to defend himself.

The effects of the potent tranquilizer immediately went to work, slowing his movement, spreading a paralyzing lassitude through his limbs. Unlike the previous shifters whom she'd caught unaware while they slept, he'd entered the cell adrenalized, so he didn't collapse to the floor in a coma-like sleep.

"You'll pay for murdering my brother," he growled as he reached out to grab her. He missed, his movement sluggish and clumsy. It seemed the drugs hit him harder than expected.

But the killer hadn't counted on his cougar. She wasn't affected at all, and with a snarled, "Bitch!", she jumped into the fray. Ricky managed a crooked grin as he slumped to his knees, an avid audience with a clear view—in duplicate—of the catfight. It wasn't even close to a fair match. Their little murderess might wield a deadly needle, but she was no match for a trained law enforcement officer with shifter strength, agility, and speed on her side. It took only a few well-aimed shots to her face to send the killing bitch reeling then one final one to the temple that made their culprit roll up her eyes and fall to the floor unconscious.

Patricia dropped to her knees in front of him. "Ricky, are you all right?"

"Fi-i-i-ne," he managed to slur with a thick tongue.

"No you're not," she grumbled. "Of all the damnable luck. I need to get this broad out of here and into council custody, but I don't want to abandon you."

"I'll come with you." He staggered to his feet. Swayed. Hit a wall, which held his weight despite the fact it spun. Actually, the whole room spun. Hmmm. Walking might be a little harder than expected until he managed to burn off some of the effects of the drug.

"You're not in any shape to help, and I can't leave you here. There will be too many questions. Nor can I lug both of you," Patricia grumbled. "I need—"

"Stu to the rescue." Wearing a grin and

nothing else, the wolf appeared at the door. For once, Ricky was kind of glad to see him, even if the damned wolf appeared twice as wide as usual—and had two sets of hanging junk, lucky bastard.

"What the heck are you doing back here?" Patricia asked.

"Funny thing happened during my little chasing game, two guards got accidentally conked on the head, dumped in a storage room, and had all their clothes stolen." He grinned. "They won't be returning to their post anytime soon, so I thought I'd see if you needed a hand, or a paw."

"Your timing is perfect because, as a matter of fact, I do need your help."

"You caught the killer?"

"In the act. And it was a she. I'll tell you about it later though. We need to move before someone comes looking. You grab Ricky while I get the girl out of here."

"What about sleeping beauty over there?" Stu jerked a thumb at the slumbering shifter with the gaping mouth and rumbling snore.

"Leave him. He has no idea he just escaped the reaper. And the fewer people with stories to tell tomorrow, the more likely our operation will go unnoticed."

"Will you be all right with the girl?"

Patricia let out a snort. "Piece of cake. I bench press more than she weighs. You just worry about getting your naked asses back to your cell before any alarms go off. Who knows when those cameras will come back online?"

Back to the cell? Ricky made a face. "Now

that we've caught her, can't we just leave?" Ricky might be fighting the sandman's lure, but his thought process still worked.

"You can't leave, not without the humans asking too many questions. Just sit tight in your cell, and as soon as I get her booked, I'll get the paperwork processed to get you moved and then wiped from the system."

"Great. Another day of prison food," Stu grumbled as he looped an arm around Ricky's upper body. With the wolf's steadying influence, they staggered their way back in the direction of their cell while Patricia, with the unconscious female slung fireman style over her shoulder, went in the opposite direction, to the outside. How she would get the killer over the wall and out without the human guards noticing, Ricky hadn't the slightest clue. Could cougars fly? He shook his head trying to clear it of the crazy thoughts. All it served to do was make everything around him distort fun-house-mirror style.

The drug cocktail coursing through his body made his drunken binges seem tame in comparison.

As they weaved the maze back to their cell, Ricky fighting off the drug through blinking eyes— while staving off the pretty floating butterflies and rainbows—Stu decided to talk.

"I see I'm not the only who got lucky today. Did you mark her?"

"No." Not for lack of wanting. Again, he cursed the timing of the inconsiderate killer. *Would it have killed her to wait five more minutes to murder?* He giggled, fucking giggled, at his unintentional pun.

"I'm surprised you're taking it so well."

"Not," he spat through numb lips, trying to ignore the bunny shadow leaping along the wall beside them.

"I guess with the case over, it's only a matter of time now before we're all joined. One big happy family. Damn. I'm never going to live this down. Me in a freakn' threesome. Do you know how much flack I gave my brothers and sister when they got involved in a three-way? This is so going to come back and bite me."

"I'm going to bite you if you don't shut up."

"Testy, testy. You're going to have to learn to curb that temper of yours if we're all going to live together. I can't see Patricia putting up with much bullshit."

"She'll whack us with her stick," Ricky agreed. Then he'd beat her with his stick. Or was that impale her with it? Either way it would—"Ouch!" Ricky couldn't help the yell as his big toe hit the edge of the door they went through.

"Shh. We don't want the guards to find us. We're almost there."

"You know, you're not all that bad for a wolf," Ricky admitted. Someone shoot him now—at least seven times since he was pretty sure that was how many lives he had left. Since when did he like the stupid wolf, and since when did he admit such a thing out loud? They'd take away his man card for sure if the news got out.

"Aah, I like you too, kitty cat."

"Call me that again, and I will ram my foot so far up your ass it will come out your mouth," Ricky growled. It came out slurred, but his intent was clear.

Not that Stu took him seriously. "I can see I'm going to have to ask Ma where she gets her sturdy furniture. I predict a few violent bumps in the road to all of us living together."

Living together? Ricky groaned. Fuck him. He'd not even thought that far ahead. The dog raised a valid point. If they both claimed Patricia, then the next step would be getting a home for all of them, which raised an interesting dilemma. "You don't think she's going to make us share a bed, do you?"

"So long as it's king sized, I think we can work it providing she stays in the middle."

"But what about when we wanna screw? Are we going to, like, take turns?"

"And what, have the other one watch? Sounds kinky."

The automatic retort was no. He expected Stu to get his ass to another room while he pleasured his woman, but on second thought, he couldn't deny a certain curiosity as to how it would feel to have an audience. Someone watching as he pleasured their cougar. Made her scream with his prowess. But how about when the wolf took his turn? Could he handle it?

Again, his first impulse was to roar a resounding no! A man did not share his woman, did not let another touch her fair skin or kiss her full lips or sink his cock into her sweet sheathe. But it seemed his body thought differently, as did his mind, because he could all too easily see the decadence of being present as his woman got taken. He'd get to watch her face as she flushed and lost herself in the grip of passion, smell her, and maybe even participate in driving her over the brink of pleasurable sanity. Could the two of them together make Patricia lose her mind with bliss?

Only one way to find out. And if it proved awkward, or he got too jealous, well, bruises eventually healed, and surely if they were mated, Patricia would forgive him for breaking her puppy's face sooner or later.

They'd almost made it back to their cell when the beam of a flashlight hit them square in the face, blinding them. Uh-oh. Ricky squinted, cursing his drunken cat, which lolled in his head and purred, not apologetic at all for not having warned him they had company approaching.

"Well, well," said a mocking voice. "What do we have here? Looks like we've got a pair of lovers out for a stroll. Hope the fucking was worth it. You're both going to solitary."

Ricky would have liked to repudiate the allegation he and Stu were lovers. However, between the drugs he still fought off and the fact Stu had dropped him to raise his hands over his head, he hit the floor face first and passed out. Buck-assed naked.

Thank god no one got it on video.

Chapter Twenty

I can't believe they got it on video.

Stunned into horrified silence, Stu watched his ignoble capture—stark naked and supporting an equally bare-assed feline—in black and white on the small screen while seated in an office rented by the shifter council. *Please don't let my brothers get a hold of this.* They'd no doubt delight in playing it at the next family gathering, probably over a big bowl of popcorn while providing a live narration.

"Bad luck about the cameras coming back online before you managed to get back to your cell," said Fred, an older wolf shifter who worked with RCMP for the jail's district. He'd been the one to bail them out of solitary a few hours before.

Bad luck indeed. Now if only they could keep it under wraps and forget the humiliation of having it played at home. With his luck, and given what he'd done to his brothers in the past, they'd probably upload it to YouTube for the world to see.

"What a shame the operation was a bust," Fred said as if unaware of the inner cringing Stu suffered as the tape repeated itself, caught in a loop of infamy.

Fred's words startled him from ways he could hack into their system and steal the master copy for destruction. He straightened in his seat, but before he could open his mouth to ask what Fred meant, Ricky uttered in a low growl, "What do you mean a bust? We caught the woman killer red-handed."

"Yes, you did. Just so you know, there seems to be no doubt as to her culpability, not judging by your reports."

"Then I don't understand. Why did you let her go?"

"We didn't. Patricia made the hand-off without any issues. What we didn't suspect was that our suspect had an accomplice."

"You're fucking kidding!" Stu couldn't help but exclaim. "None of the facts in the cases hinted at the possibility." But, then again, given the intricacy required in getting in and out, not to mention staging the murderous events, should have tipped them off. Stu slammed his head down on the desk for not even thinking of it.

Fred reiterated his thoughts. "No one suspected a second villain, and yet, there's no disguising the fact that someone followed Patricia after she took the killer into custody and got her out of the prison. After she made the exchange, the acquiring agent, while sitting at a red light, was shot through the windshield multiple times. The second assailant probably assumed he'd die. He didn't by the way, but while the agent was incapacitated, the woman in custody was freed. She and her partner have since vanished."

Stu wanted to slam his head against the desk again. Instead he asked in a morose voice, "So they're both back out there? And in possession of our secret?"

"Afraid so. As you might imagine, the council is quite upset by this turn of events."

"Are you putting us back undercover to see if

they'll come back to the prison? Do you want us to cover another prison?" Ricky asked, immediately volunteering them.

"Thanks for the offer, but no. Your cover is compromised. If the killers see you, they'll just move on. Your role in this is over, gentlemen."

"What do you mean over? There's still a pair of shifter killers out there. We can help you catch them." Ricky said what Stu didn't. He thought it though.

I might not have ever thought of myself as a fighter for justice, but this killing duo needs to be stopped. They can't be allowed to continue killing shifters. Not to mention, Ricky needed closure. Stu knew about his brother's death. *If it were one of my brothers, I wouldn't want to rest until the culprit was caught.*

"Thanks but no thanks. We already have several teams on the job. The suspects have been identified via fingerprint. It's only a matter of time before they surface, and when they do, we'll get them. You are free to go back to your lives. As a thanks for your service, the shifter council has deposited monetary sums to your bank accounts."

With those final words and a handshake to thank them for doing this civic shifter duty, Fred left them with more questions than answers. But Ricky wasn't afraid to shout the most important one, "What about Patricia? Where is she? We need to talk to her."

Fred paused and turned back to look at them. "Patricia has taken a leave of absence."

'What? She wouldn't have left the case with those monsters at large."

"She wasn't given a choice. She was also compromised. Given that she hates desk work, she decided to cash in some of her vacation days."

"So she's home."

"Not that I know of."

"You mean she's left? She can't have. We need to talk to her." More than talk. The three of them needed to resolve the mating issue once and for all.

Fred shook his head. "Sorry. Anything you need to say will have to wait until she gets back."

Ricky loomed over the other man, bristling from every pore, his eyes flashing golden as his cat showed its irritation at being thwarted. "We can't wait that long. We need to know where she is now."

It didn't intimidate Fred in the least. "I'm afraid we can't divulge private info about another agent."

"The woman is our mate."

"Not according to her file."

"Because we were waiting to solve the case to exchange the mating mark."

"And it looks like you'll have to wait a bit longer. I wish I could help you, but the boss would have my ass if I gave out info on another agent. Sorry, boys." With an apologetic shrug, Fred left.

Ricky slammed the table with a fist. "Bloody freakn' hell. All that bullshit in the prison was for nothing."

"Not completely for nothing. We now know at least who one of the killers is. And because of the prison food, I lost a few pounds and fit in my jeans from high school again."

The glare Ricky shot his way almost singed his skin.

But Stu had survived dirtier looks from his siblings. "Hey, do you know how much vintage Levi's cost? I'm in pants heaven."

"I can't believe you're acting so blasé about the fact that our mate essentially ran away."

"She went to clear her head."

"Alone. Who knows when and if she'll come back? Doesn't that bother you in the slightest?"

"Not really, because I know where she is."

Years of living with four other brothers had given Stu special abilities. It came in handy in moments like these when he needed to duck a body flying through the air, intent on a headlong tackle. Had he goaded the cat? Damned straight he had. Just because Stu had to partner with Ricky didn't mean he couldn't have fun. Even if that fun came with a few lumps and bruises.

It was just like being at home.

Chapter Twenty-One

Cowardly. Not a word Patricia had ever used to describe herself, yet it was the path she'd chosen when her mission ended and the shifter council informed her she was free to return to her life. Just one problem; she no longer knew what that life was, or with who.

Her first act as an egg-laying fowl? She

handed off the task of freeing Stu and Ricky to someone else. Distance made her body ache. Separation from them made her anxious. Those two combined scared her poor, battered heart. So she ran back to Ottawa, back to her home.

It should have proven easy to slip back into her old job and apartment. Okay, maybe not easy. Putting the mission behind her while knowing a killer and an accomplice still roamed left a hairball in her throat, but Patricia's role was done, whether she liked it or not. *Time to tackle a new job.* It was what she usually did no matter the outcome. Report to work, accept whatever duty her boss assigned her, and do it to the best of her ability.

Yeah, that didn't happen.

For one thing, she couldn't stop thinking about the fact a pair of someones targeted her kind. They needed to be captured. But her bigger dilemma was she couldn't stop thinking of Stu and Ricky. How she missed them. How she wanted to see them. How it would never work.

Setting foot in her apartment back in Ottawa, she expected to shed some of the anxiety she'd lived with over the past while. Instead, she couldn't help but notice the quiet, the stillness, how lonely her home appeared. Sterile walls still painted a dull beige. No pictures or color to adorn them. A single comfortable armchair in front of her flat screen television, which sat propped on a pair of unopened boxes. Boxes of memories and knickknacks she couldn't bear to part with yet couldn't stand to see in the open.

This wasn't the home of a person who lived

or enjoyed life. This wasn't a place of happiness and laughter. Not a place of love or sharing. It was a blatant admission that she'd never moved on or gotten over Ryker's untimely death. Worse, it was a slap in his face, to his memory, because she knew, knew with every ounce of her being, that he wouldn't have wanted this for her. That he would have been the first to tell her to get on with her damned life, to not live in the past, and to embrace the present and dream of a bright future.

A future with someone else.

The truth hit her in the face, and still she couldn't face it, couldn't accept it, and for the second time in as many days, she ran away from a problem instead of facing it. She bolted like a frightened animal to the one place that never failed to ground her, her grandfather's cabin in the Rockies.

This late in the fall, she arrived to a blanket of white as snow covered the ground and roof of the rustic, log-hewn cabin. She punched in the code on the keypad to let herself in and stomped her booted feet on the mat to knock off the snow before slipping her footwear off. She padded into the comfortable setting in her thick wool socks, the plank floor smoothed by sanding and years of use, chilly even through that thermal layer.

With cold fingers, she set some pieces of wood in the potbellied woodstove, balling up some leftover newspapers to provide a quick kindling for the match she lit. Flames whooshed, crackling and dancing, consuming the dry tinder and exhaling heat into the frigid room. Slamming the heavy metal door shut to prevent stray sparks, she stood and looked around.

The moment she'd entered, tension eased from her shoulders. This place never failed to soothe. Everywhere she looked there were happy memories. The rocking chair in the corner where her granddaddy used to snuggle her on his lap, regaling her with stories of the bears he'd hunted in his prime. The worn couch with the sagging springs, covered in an afghan knitted by her mother. She could remember so many occasions where she and her parents, or she and Ryker, had sat on those cushions, laughing and cuddling. Tears pricked her eyes.

I was once so happy. Until everyone she loved left her. Was it any wonder she'd fled Ricky and Stu before they could get any closer? She'd gone through so much loss already. She didn't have it in her to do it again.

Let them move on to someone else. Surely the mating fever would die off the longer she stayed away. Surely fate and nature would give the guys a second chance.

But what about me?

She'd had her moment in the sun. Time for them to get theirs. She didn't allow the warmth of their smiles, the remembrance of their touch, to intrude on her thoughts. She couldn't allow it because, if she did, then she'd begin to doubt her decision and the path she'd chosen for herself, that of a single cougar, living out her life, alone.

It sounded so pathetic. So woe is me. What had happened to the brave woman she used to be? The one who feared nothing, most especially not life and love?

Rubbing her eyes, she strode back to the door and grabbed her knapsack. She carried it into her bedroom and tossed it on the bed before her gaze was snagged by something on her nightstand. Overcome, she sank to her knees before the one personal item in the room. *How could I have forgotten this was here?* It was an image of Ryker, hair tousled as he smiled at the camera, so happy. Her heart wrenched.

She couldn't help the mournful wail that she uttered, a howl not just from her human self but her cat. Seeing his face again, she realized something she'd tried to avoid. She had to face reality.

Ryker is gone. He's not coming back.

And it was time for her to let him go. Again. Sure she'd done it once, when he died, and she'd adjusted to living alone, sleeping alone, getting through each day without him at her side. But now, she needed to set him free a second time because it was time to let his memory rest in peace. *It's time for me to stop pitying my luck and to resume living.*

Yes, she would always miss Ryker. She would never forget the man who was her mate. But she couldn't live in limbo forever. It wasn't making her happy. It certainly wouldn't have made Ryker happy, and it definitely didn't make Stu or Ricky happy.

She needed to move on to the next stage of her life. But before she did, she allowed herself a good long cry and got drunk because, dammit, she needed it.

Tipsy, and cried out, she found herself in need of a vigorous shaking up. She stripped down and stepped forth from the cabin, naked as the day of her birth. She raised her arms to the starlit sky, the cool air pebbling her skin.

"Goodbye, Ryker." As she shifted forms and loped off into the woods, the snow puffing in little clouds by her feet, she could almost swear she felt his ghostly presence running alongside her, approving of her decision. With each cleansing step she took, with each lungful of burning, cold air she inhaled, she felt stronger. The guilt she'd allowed to burden her, melted.

Living again was the right choice. Loving again was not a betrayal. She could be happy. She could teach her young suitors to love eighties music and not make her feel old by calling it retro. She could learn to play Stu's video games. She could help Ricky on his mission to save youths.

She could do it all. If she let them claim her.

Which was kind of hard for them to do given she'd run off to hide in the middle of nowhere without telling a soul.

Come to think of it, that might not have been her brightest move, especially given the killers she'd hunted had gotten loose.

But surely they wouldn't have followed her to the mountains. The missing perps had a very clear itinerary when it came to their murders. However, given she and her boys had thrown that plan into chaos, would they change their modus operandi and switch tactics? Could she and her young lovers become targets?

Are Ricky and Stu in danger?

The very thought stopped her in her snowy tracks. Her sides heaved, and her breath steamed the air as she realized her selfishness and cowardice might have left her mates vulnerable. *They need me.* Someone needed her. She had to get back!

Anyone watching might have wondered at the massive golden cougar that did an abrupt one eighty and sped back in the direction she came from. She sped through the shadows, dodging branches that sought to dump their icy loads of flakes on her. Muscles in her legs tensed and bunched for power as she leapt over snow-covered obstacles. Faster. Faster. She needed to get back. Urgency drove her.

Logic dictated she could do nothing this night, not even leave the mountain, because only the suicidal attempted to drive the winding, twisting road in the pitch black, especially in these types of icy conditions. Knowing she couldn't travel back to her lovers and mates until morning didn't slow her pace, and her less-than-careful flight brought attention. An ululating howl split the crisp air off to her right and not far off. It sounded again, and her cougar emitted a chuffing growl as it recognized the call of a wolf.

More voices joined in, the call of the lone hunter answered by a pack. Shit. Given she knew of no shifter packs in these environs, that could only mean one thing. Unenlightened, feral wolves. Great. And if there was one thing a pack of wolves hated, it was kitty cats encroaching on their territory.

One-on-one, she could take on a wild canine, even two, but add in a couple or more and she was royally screwed unless she could make it to her cabin first. There she could barricade herself behind the thick log walls and, with the aide of granddad's shotgun, pick them off if needed.

But the wolves proved closer than expected. Branches crackled around her. The sharp yips of their excitement echoed much too close. As she raced through the snow, sides heaving with exertion, she strove to pour every ounce of energy she possessed into escaping. She also couldn't help but curse her own foolishness in running away from her problems.

If she'd stayed and faced her fears, she wouldn't now be alone, about to fight to live. How ironic. She'd just come to the subconscious realization that she'd not been living, and now she had to fight in the real world to actually get that chance.

The wolves flanked her, their sleek fur blending with shadows as they paced alongside her, their yellow eyes glinting as they eyed her with slavering delight. When one veered too close in an attempt to nip at her, without slowing her pace, she snarled and swiped. She missed. However the daring wolf lost his footing in his attempt to dodge her claws and tumbled into the powdery snow.

Not far now ...

She burst from the tree line into the clearing she kept around the cottage. Starlight barely lit the space, but the snow sparkled as it picked up the faint illumination. It also outlined the shape of the really large wolf standing in its midst smack-dab between her and the door to safety.

Of all the bad luck! She skidded on the snowy ground, the slick ice under the fluffy layer not slowing her momentum. She braced herself for impact. Hackles rose along her spine. Her lip pulled back over pointed teeth in a snarl. She wouldn't give in without a fight.

A shift in the wind brought the scent of the wolf to her nose, and her ferocious stance turned to one of surprise as she recognized it.

Stu!

He'd come for her! Her young mate and lover, whom she had so ignobly ditched, had tracked her down. And he'd not come alone.

The front door to her cottage flung open, and a tall shape filled it. Not for long. Ricky's transformation happened in a blink of an eye. A fierce yowl pierced the air as a black shadow bounded from her cottage, the indoor light illuminating the panther's sleek frame before Ricky melted into the pockets of darkness.

It seemed the suitors she'd thought to escape had found her.

And, lucky her, they'd arrived just in time to play.

Chapter Twenty-Two

Of all the things Stu and Ricky expected to find when they showed up at the remote cabin, which he'd found only after some fancy—and, ahem, illegal—searches of online databases, it wasn't to see his beloved cougar racing at him with a pack of wolves at her thrashing tail.

What a sweetheart. She'd brought his beast some toys to play with. While human Stu might lack a certain grace and finesse, his wolf side was all about the hunt. With a mighty howl, which echoed only seconds after Ricky's feline one, Stu dove at his distant cousins who dared threaten his mate.

Fur and teeth met in a clash. Snarls and yips broke the stillness of the wintry night. Six wolves had dared to attack, but against an even bigger wolf and two large cats, they didn't stand a chance. While the felines swiped with their deadly claws, leaving bleeding furrows, Stu preferred to grab his opponents by the scruff of their necks and shake them. It didn't take long before the pack realized the futility of their attack.

With whimpers, and most of them limping, they blended back into the shadows of the forest, leaving behind two fallen comrades who hadn't survived the short, yet vicious, battle.

Stu sat on his haunches in the trampled snow and let loose a howl of triumph, one cut short as a very naked woman threw herself against him and looped her arms around his furry neck for a hug.

"I can't believe you came," Patricia exclaimed before she buried her face in his fur.

While Scooby Doo never had a problem articulating himself, Stu had never quite managed the trick of talking while in wolf form. He shifted shapes, ignoring for the moment the chilly ground against his nude flesh in favor of the warm and pleasurable sensation of his skin against Patricia's.

"Of course I came. We came," he corrected. "You didn't really think we'd let you escape that easily, did you?"

"I wasn't really thinking at all."

"Obviously," retorted Ricky as he strode up and tugged Patricia away from Stu to give her a hug of his own. "No way were we letting you run away. Whatever the problem is, we'll work through it. Even if it means waiting," Ricky grimaced, "or sharing you with the hairy puppy."

Patricia laughed. "So despite this," she reached down and gripped Ricky's cock, semi-erect even in the chill air, "and this," she plastered her mouth to his in a kiss that roused Stu's jealous beast only a bit, "you'd let me walk away if I said I needed more time?"

Poor Ricky. His pained look made Stu snicker. "I think she's joking, partner."

"Of course I am. Even I'm not so cruel."

A shiver wracked Ricky's body. "I don't know. You seem intent on having a heart-to-heart in the godforsaken freezing cold. Can't we go inside before we have a serious discussion? Maybe lie in front of a warm fire before my male parts get frostbite and fall off?"

"I hear the best way to warm up is skin to skin," she replied. "Coming?" She tossed a coy look and a smile over her shoulder at Stu.

Coming? Damned straight he was, hopefully in something wet and tight.

He sprang to his feet and clasped his fingers in the ones she extended. Hand in hand, Ricky flanking her other side, they made their way barefoot on the crunching snow to the still-open front door.

Once inside, the warmth from the fireplace blasted them, the heat intense after the extreme cold of the outdoors. Ricky wasted no time in scooping a spot in front of the roaring fire, sitting cross-legged on the massive bear rug laid before it.

"I hope that thing wasn't related to Ethan," he muttered, knowing his brother-in-law had family in these parts.

Again, Patricia delighted his senses with laughter. "No, this isn't from a shifter. Just a regular old grizzly. My granddad shot him back in the eighties after tracking him for over a week. He was harassing some of the humans and sniffing around some grizzly shifter females. Granddad said he was the biggest he'd ever seen."

Judging by the width and length of the pelt, Stu would have to agree.

Seeing a slight shiver run through her frame, Stu grabbed the soft fleece blanket hanging on the arm of the couch and draped it around her shoulders.

"Come here where it's warm." Ricky gestured to the fire. His skin had lost its bluish hue, and he leaned back, a teasing grin on his lips. When Ricky opened his arms and gestured to his lap, she sank into it. Stu might have gotten a little envious had she not turned a smile his way and patted the spot beside them. He sank down on the rug, the fur ticking his backside. She draped her legs over his in a gesture of intimacy he appreciated, showing he was part of whatever would happen next.

Unfortunately, it proved to be talk and not sex.

"I'm glad you guys found me because I want to apologize," she said, ducking her head so that her blonde bob covered her features. "It was wrong of me to just leave you guys in the lurch after everything that happened between us."

"You got scared. It happens." Or so Stu's mother had explained to him when he went home moping and complaining about his broken heart.

Actually their exact conversation went more along the lines of:

"Did you expect it to be easy? The poor girl had her heart torn out when her mate died. It's a wonder she even contemplated taking you on, let alone another pig-headed male."

"But she's our mate, Ma. I thought once you met the one, it was supposed to be, I don't know, like instant love and happily ever after."

He didn't duck the gentle smack she aimed his way. "Idiot. And I thought you were the smart one after your sister. The mating fever only helps you to recognize each other. To show your compatibility. It doesn't suddenly change a person. It doesn't make them fall madly in love, especially in this case, where Patricia already had a mate. She's dealing with a lot of emotions right about now. I'll bet guilt is a big one, but even stronger than that is fear. She's scared of letting herself care again. Right now, she's probably thinking that if she does let herself mate with you or this Ricky fellow, that she runs the risk of facing heartbreak all over again if something happens to you."

"So what am I supposed to do?"

"Give her room. Let her realize on her own that happiness is worth taking a chance."

"Kind of hard for her to come to that conclusion if she never has to see us again."

"Idiot. I've raised an idiot," his mother lamented, lifting her eyes to the ceiling. "When I said give her room, I didn't mean don't find her."

"Are you saying I should go after her?"

"Of course you should. The sooner, the better. Give her your support. Give her your love.

Give her my body.

He yelped at his mother's smack upside the head. "Hey, what was that for?"

"I'm giving you good advice, and your mind is in the gutter."

He rubbed the sore spot and scowled. "I don't know why I come to you for help."

"Because I never steer you wrong. Now get your shaggy ass onto that computer of yours and track her down. Be sure to bring along that other fellow once you do find her."

"Do I have to?" he whined. "Can't I leave him behind?"

"No. Fate has said she needs both of you. So be a man, and do what's best for her. Or else."

He couldn't resist asking. "Or else what?"

"Or else a certain video taken in prison is going to end up emailed to someone's brothers."

Evil mother. Who needed size and strength to win

battles when wily wickedness was so much more effective?

Patricia shifted on Ricky's lap so she could face both of them. "I was a coward," she said bluntly. "I let my fear of getting hurt dictate my actions."

"Is it me, or am I sensing something changed your mind?" Ricky replied, his hands disappearing under the blanket to stroke her skin. Or so Stu assumed. He massaged her calves, letting his hands inch slowly up her leg.

"I got here and had an epiphany. I was already miserable. I was living in the past, letting my fear of caring again chain me. By refusing a chance at happiness and a future with you both, I was creating my own unhappiness. Does that make any sense? Because it sounded a lot more coherent in my head." She uttered a wry laugh.

Stu's hands worked past her knee to her thigh. "Perfect sense. It's why we're here. We knew you needed to figure out that you couldn't hold on to the past. But, at the same time, we wanted to be here. To be here for you so you could get a glimpse of the future. We only want to make you happy."

"Very happy," Ricky purred, placing a kiss on her neck.

"I know that, but are you sure? I mean, not only do I have emotional scars, you do realize I'm older than you, right? I'm not some young twenty-year-old who's going to be able to pop out a half dozen babies. Not to mention I have a career and—"

Ricky silenced her protests with a kiss. The intimacy of it should have freaked Stu out. Perhaps even roused his jealousy. Instead it felt right.

This was how it was meant to be. The three of

them, together, a team against the world. A male duo made for a cougar.

Not to be left out, Stu leaned forward and placed a kiss on her thigh. He heard her gasp and felt the tremble that went through her body.

"What happens next?" she asked in a shaky voice.

"Now we make love to you," Ricky stated.

"Every gorgeous inch," Stu added.

"The two of you at once?" Patricia squeaked.

"Can you think of a better way to celebrate the future?" Ricky asked.

"But I've never— I mean—"

Stu kissed his way up her thigh, close enough to inhale the rich musk of her arousal. "Neither have we. We'll learn together."

Having his lover seated on another man's lap while he teased the skin of her thighs proved interesting, especially since Stu could hear the sound of them kissing, but he didn't feel like a third wheel, not when her fingers drifted to the crown of his head to sift through strands of his hair. She also squirmed at his touch, parting her thighs to give him a glimpse of the pink nirvana he couldn't wait to taste.

Placing soft butterfly kisses on her legs, he used his hand to stroke through her blonde curls until he found her sweet spot. Dipping a finger into the nectar glistening on her sex, he rubbed her clit and knew she enjoyed it by the way she gripped his hair.

He'd almost forgotten there was third player involved until Ricky said in a gruff voice, "Lick her sweet pussy."

For real? The command by another guy should have thrown him for a loop. Instead, his already throbbing arousal grew thicker. To aid him with his verbal order, Ricky leaned back, pulling Patricia with him so she reclined against his chest. Ricky used the couch to brace himself, leaving his hands free to cup her beautiful breasts. The sight of her, eyes closed, lips parted, her perfect globes stroked by tanned hands, tweaking and rolling the nipples, was an erotic sight.

Forget watching an erotic video. This was voyeurism in living 3D, color, sound, and smell.

However, even better than watching, he could touch. He dipped down for a lick, a simple flick of his tongue across the pink pussy that beckoned. Mmm. A burst of musky flavor on his tongue, a quiver of her flesh, and a sweet sigh parting her lips.

"Lick her again," Ricky murmured. "And, this time, don't stop until she creams herself."

Damn, how another guy giving the orders could prove such a turn-on he didn't care to analyze, but Stu did as told and went in for another taste. This time, he latched onto her, stabbing his tongue between her velvety folds while his thumb rubbed against her clit. Good thing he had help in holding her down. She thrashed like a wild cat caught in a trap, a sensual one wrought of pleasure and teasing. Emboldened despite his audience, Stu devoted himself to his decadent feast and, in the midst of pleasuring his woman, let his gaze stray to what happened above him. A visual sensory delighted awaited, especially for a man who'd recently discovered the pleasures of voyeurism.

Ricky's fingers thrummed the erect peaks of Patricia's breasts, stroking the hard points. His lips were buried against the column of her neck, nuzzling and sucking. When he finally released his hold, a red mark stood in sharp contrast against her pale skin, not quite a mating mark, but a sign she belonged to them.

Stu hummed his approval, a vibration that sent shockwaves through her already quivering body. He continued to lap at her sex, a steady rhythm that had her panting and mewling, but he could tell his tongue and Ricky's caresses weren't enough. She needed more to fly over the edge. He shifted his focus and let his lips capture the nub of her clit while, at the same time, thrusting two then three fingers into her tight sheath.

He just about came as her channel squeezed him tight, a vise-like grip that he couldn't wait to feel on his cock.

"That's it," Ricky crooned, watching with smoldering eyes. "Finger fuck her while you lick. Make her come. Make her scream. Show her the pleasure only we can give."

Again, he hummed his approval, loving how she cried out at the extra stimulation. Faster, he thrust his fingers, knowing she approached the brink from the whimpering cadence of her cries and the bucking of her body. When her climax hit, he had an up-close view and taste. So gloriously beautiful.

He continued to lap at her, even after she came down from her orgasm, delighting in the aftershocks. He could have kept going had she not pushed at him with a huskily spoken, "Enough.

You're going to kill me. Besides, I think it's about time I took care of you both."

Shaggy and shy Stu might have an uttered a "Zoinks", but almost-mated Stu's response as he scrabbled to accommodate was more of a "Hell yeah!"

As for Ricky? His reply was an eloquent, "Come and suck me, *bebé*."

To Stu's surprise, instead of a slap or a painful ripping off of Ricky's dick, Patricia, with a purred "my pleasure" crawled up between his legs, giving Stu a bird's-eye view of her pussy, pink, glistening and oh so tempting.

Sweet freakn' hell. Despite having just indulged in its bounty, it called to him, begged him to now partake in dessert. Her musky scent surrounded him in a seductive cloud, and he couldn't help but grip his cock and stroke it. Stroke it and practically pant in excitement as he watched her head dip so she could lick the tip of Ricky's cock. This had the effect of pushing her buttocks even farther in the air as she let her spine curve so she could rest her elbows on Ricky thighs, a brace to hold her aloft as she proceeded to gift Ricky with a blowjob. And she didn't just give him a bj; she enjoyed it. She purred and undulated her body as she took Ricky's thick cock into her mouth and sucked.

Even though he wasn't the one on the receiving end, Stu enjoyed his role of spectator. The way her head bobbed in a steady rhythm. Her enthusiastic suck and the hollowness of her cheeks. The way her pussy clenched before his very eyes, just as happy to give oral as receive it.

Had there ever been a woman more perfect?

Wanting to be a part of the unfolding decadence, Stu spread her cheeks, exposing her to his gaze. She was so ready. The cream of her arousal glistened on her tender flesh, and as he stared, she wiggled in clear invitation. His cock, thicker and longer than he'd ever imagined, strained and pulsed. Stu slapped the fat head of it off her clit. She arched and cried out, losing, for a moment, her bobbing rhythm.

Stu tapped her cleft again with his dick, but this time when she bucked, he rammed his cock into her channel, lightning quick. Just as rapidly, he withdrew it and smacked her swollen nub again.

Ricky watched with glowing eyes and growled in approval. "Slap her again. Harder this time."

With pleasure. Again and again, Stu smacked his shaft off her pussy, and before she'd done quivering, he slammed himself into her, gasping as her muscles flexed and squeezed him. It felt so freakn' good. So good he feared blowing his load too quick. But he had to hold on, had to wait until she came first.

"Stop teasing me," snarled Patricia, tossing him a wild look over her shoulder. "Fuck me. Hard. Fast. And—"

Whatever else she planned to say got cut off as Stu pistoned into her, hips pumping in wild abandon, building friction, fighting the suctioning pull of her pussy. When she came, she screamed, and her sex pulsed around him, so tight he lost his rhythm and held himself still inside her, basking in the strength of her orgasm.

Before the waves shuddering through her channel could calm down, he began thrusting again, in and out, in and out, a quick tempo. The urge to bite her became almost overpowering. The need to make her his almost made him forget his vow to wait. At the last minute, sanity prevailed, and he pulled out to come all over her lower back in a hot rush.

He collapsed beside her on the carpet, panting and recovering with a bird's eye view as she calmed down from her orgasm and proceeded to take care of Ricky's still-swollen dick.

She gave new meaning to the term deep throating. Her lips slid down the thick cock, all the way down until she touched the base. Then up she slid, her cheeks deep hollows as she suctioned with fervor. Ricky's fingers fisted her hair, and he encouraged her as he guided her in a cadence on his cock.

"That's it, *bebé*. Suck me. Take all of my hard cock in your mouth. Such a greedy girl. Such a good girl."

Any other time, Patricia might have taken offense. She wasn't a submissive woman by nature, but here and now, in private with Ricky giving her orders, taking on the role of dominant, she listened—and obeyed. Even better, she enjoyed.

The sound of her purring exceeded that of her sucking, a deep vibration that surely felt wonderful on Ricky's cock. Stu hoped he'd inspire the same pleasure when his turn to have her lips on him came. He'd love to know what it felt like to have that rumble on his dick.

Faster and faster, she worked Ricky's cock, her hand aiding now by fisting the base while she concentrated on the sensitive tip. With a yell that was more primal cat roar than man, Ricky came in her mouth, and their greedy cougar took it all, even lapped at the swollen head, looking for more.

Damn.

Everyone satisfied for the moment, she leaned back on her haunches and, with a grin to rival the cat who swallowed the canary, said, "Meow."

Ricky arched a brow in query. "Meow?"

Her grinned stretched wider. "Isn't that what a kitty should say after great sex?"

"No, she should be saying thank you."

Stu's jaw wasn't the only one that dropped at Ricky's temerity. Then he saw the mischievous wink. And when Patricia dove on Ricky to retaliate for his remark, Stu joined in on the fun. When it came to tickle torture, he knew all the spots.

And when it came to pinning the loser to give her the ultimate tickle, in the form of Ricky's cock pumping between her thighs, his earlier wish came true.

Purring blowjobs did feel even better than they looked.

Chapter Twenty-Three

The morning after wasn't as awkward as expected. Patricia awoke beside only one male body, probably because her other lover had wandered off to the kitchen to make some breakfast, or so her twitching nose indicated as the scent of sizzling bacon roused her taste buds and set her tummy rumbling.

At her side slumbered Stu, one arm thrown over her waist, the warm solid presence of his body pressing along her length. It almost made her blush to remember what they'd done the night before.

I made love to two men at once. And it was love. She might have hesitated last night to let them place the mating mark, but there was no denying it in the light of day. Without meaning to, and despite the obstacles she feared, these two men had come to mean so much to her. They'd brought light and love back into her life. They'd also managed to eradicate the guilt that came with her acceptance of happiness.

She could almost feel Ryker's approval cocooning her from wherever his spirit resided now. She mouthed a silent thank you for this second chance. She also wondered when would be the best time to tell her guys she was ready. She slid out of bed and tossed on some comfortable pants and a shirt.

Stu yawned and stretched in bed, an almost silly smile creasing his lips as he announced, "Good morning."

"Yes it is." She smiled back.

"What's the plan for today?" he asked, throwing back the covers and standing, his body arching into a stretch that caught her gaze and roused a carnal hunger.

Telling you both I love you. Definitely. It was time for her to face the future. The question was when and how? She pondered that question as she wandered out of the bedroom, lured by the scent of food. Should she wait for a romantic moment? Maybe just blurt it out over breakfast in between bites of the fluffy pancakes Ricky whipped up? Not a bad plan, especially once she saw the potential for fun and sweetness with the bottle of syrup.

But before she could announce her decision, Ricky said, "About time you lazy asses got out of bed."

"Not my fault someone worked us over hard," Stu teased.

To her shock, she actually blushed which of course made them both chuckle. Ducking her head, she plopped her butt down on a chair and eyed the scratched surface of the table, ignoring them. Not an easy task given the intimate setting and the fact their scent curled around her, wrapping her in yummy testosterone. The guys each took a seat, flanking her, pressing their thighs against hers. Making her so aware. So—

She shook her head, trying to clear it of the erotic thoughts filling it. Surely she had more control than this. She tilted her chin at a stubborn angle and ignored them as she piled food on to her plate. Four fluffy pancakes, drowned in syrup, a few crispy strips of bacon and a tall glass of orange juice. The perfect meal to replenish her energy after a night of decadence. The perfect meal to give her the calories needed for a morning of strenuous exercise. The quicker the better. She fell on the scrumptious breakfast with gusto ignoring their amused looks.

"Hungry?" Ricky asked unable to completely mask his mirth.

"Starving," she purred, flicking him a coy look. Syrup coated her lips and she licked them. She didn't miss either of the smoldering looks aimed her way.

"Before we indulge in that *hunger*," Ricky said with a wink. "First we need to refuel. Bellies and the woodstove. One of us needs to get more wood. We're getting low."

"No problem. Since you cooked, I'll get more logs for the fire," Stu offered, wiping his mouth with a napkin before standing. A shame, she would have loved to lick the stickiness from his lips. "Where is the wood pile?"

"Around the back of the cabin, there's a lean-to. It's under the tarp." Despite only making it to the cabin sporadically, Patricia paid a guy in the little town at the bottom of the mountain to keep the cabin stocked with split logs. The weather this high up could prove unpredictable, and only an idiot would stay somewhere without a decent supply. Despite being surrounded by a forest, only chopped and cured lumber really worked well for burning. Everything else was too damp and produced more smoke than heat.

"Back in a jiffy." Wearing only a pair of low-slung jeans and boots with no socks, Stu exited the cabin, leaving her alone with Ricky.

It seemed her decision to have her guys claim her would have to wait a little while longer. *I wonder if I can fit them both in the shower with me and bite them first?*

Mmm. Just the thought of the water sluicing over their bodies, slipping and sliding over hers while her mouth chose a decadent spot for a nibble sent a quiver through her frame.

"Penny for your thoughts?" Ricky offered as he cleared the table.

Rising from her seat, she grabbed the empty plates and brought them to the sink. "Why so cheap?"

"I have a feeling I already know what you're thinking, which means I need to save every dime I have for the future."

"And why do you think you're going to require a large sum? Planning something, are you?"

"You tell me." He turned so he leaned against the woodblock countertop, his shirtless torso a distracting temptation.

She held him off but couldn't stop a coy grin. "We should wait for Stu to return. He'll probably want to hear this—"

Bang!

The sharp crack of a gun saw them both moving; Ricky for the front door, her for the service revolver, which she kept in its holster hanging on the coat rack. Her mind whirled with possible scenarios. Hunters? Rare in this area but possible. Of more concern, had the lone shot hit Stu? She hadn't heard him cry out, but was that because he wasn't hurt or because he'd gone down?

A blast of icy air hit her as Ricky raced out into the chill morning while she pulled her gun free. A second then a third shot fired, the last one aimed straight through the open door and embedding itself in the log wall by her head and sending out a splatter of splinters.

Well, that answered one question. *Someone is trying to kill us.* Whoever wielded the weapon did so intentionally. Ducking down, she crab-walked over to the window in a wide berth that kept her out of sight of the open front door. Revolver gripped tight, she eased herself high enough to peer over the window ledge. The brilliance of the sun reflecting on snow initially blinded her, and she blinked several times to dissipate the glare.

When she could finally see, she couldn't help her gasp of dismay. Face down in the snow, a snow tainted with red, laid Ricky. He didn't move, and she had to bite the inside of her cheek to tamp down her initial impulse to run out and check on him.

She'd do neither of them any good if she got herself shot. Turning her focus away from him, she scanned the perimeter of the yard, paying special attention to the tree line and the hiding spaces within. At first, she saw nothing. Then, there behind a snowy bush, a hint of movement. She held her breath and watched.

The rustle came again, dislodging some of the snow from the bush's limbs, and part of a body dressed in a white snowsuit leaned into view. The face, obscured by a white ski mask and goggles, peeked out, along with the edge of a rifle.

Someone had come prepared. Ricky chose that moment to move, rolling over onto his back with a loud groan. Blood streaked his skin, making it hard to see where his injury was. Didn't matter though. Anger burned in Patricia. How dare someone shoot him on her turf? Just when she'd decided to let herself care. Just when she'd finally found happiness.

And it seemed the attacker wasn't content to just injure. Out he strode from the cover of the trees, rifle aimed at her defenseless lover. Ready to finish him off.

Like freakn' hell.

Snarling on the inside, but stone cold deadly on the outside, Patricia let her law enforcement training take over. She dove and rolled for the front door, aiming as she landed.

Crack!

The single shot hit its mark, and red blossomed on the chest of the attacker. Given the situation, Patricia hadn't aimed to wound. She'd been in too many life-or-death situations to make that mistake. A wounded perp was the most dangerous, an armed and hurting one even worse. She shot to kill, and her training didn't forsake her. With a cold detachment earned from years of missions, both for humans and shifters, she watched the results of her handiwork.

For a moment, the figure stood, a statue all in white except for the blossoming stain of red, it's brightness a deadly unfurling flower. In spite of the mask over the eyes, she could almost see the moment the realization of their mortality hit. The surprise.

The disbelief. The fear.

The gun dropped from suddenly numb fingers. The attacker sank to his knees. For a moment he wavered, mouth opening and shutting without emitting a sound. Death arrived on silent wings, and the gunman pitched forward into the snow.

Then, and only then, did Patricia race out to check on Ricky.

And she almost lost her life.

Chapter Twenty-Four

Whistling and on top the world, Stu had exited the cabin, feeling like the world's luckiest wolf. As he trudged around the cabin in fluffy snow, he couldn't help but grin in remembrance of the previous night.

What a night. Patricia might not have claimed him or Ricky as mates yet, but she was close. So close.

As a matter of fact, given the way she'd eyed them both over breakfast—like juicy steaks she couldn't wait to take a bite from—Stu had to wonder if by lunchtime today he wouldn't be a mated man. Hot damn, he hoped so.

Forget the single life. He was ready to start something new. Leave the den he'd grown up in and share his future with the hottest cougar around. Heck, he'd even come to enjoy the company of the mangy cat he'd have to share her with. His computer programming business could be done from anywhere. So moving out wouldn't prove a chore, although, if her apartment was small, they might have to get a bigger—

His wolf growled inside his head, and he paused in stacking the wood in his arms. *Never ignore the instincts of your beast.* His dad's advice, repeated over the years, had him listening to the silence.

Shit. He hit the ground a moment before the whistle of a bullet whizzed past his head and embedded itself in the woodpile behind him.

Forests were never quiet, even in the winter, unless something disturbed its denizens. And someone with a gun definitely counted as disturbing. What didn't make sense though was them shooting at Stu. It wasn't as if he wore his wolf. So who the heck had followed them out here intent on taking potshots?

Sharp on the heels of that observation was an urge to call out to Patricia and tell her to take cover because, knowing her, she'd heard the gunfire and would come to his rescue. But shouting would reveal his location to the gunman and the fact he'd missed. Then, again, he probably already knew that if he watched.

Dilemma. Reassure Patricia and give away his status and position or stay silent and risk her putting herself in harm's way? The decision was taken from him.

A second shot echoed in the air, and his heart missed a beat, especially once he realized it came from a second source.

Damn it. There are two of them!

What to do. Pinned as he was, and weaponless, what could he do to help? A third shot rang out, again from the front of the cottage, and he saw movement in the woods as a figure dressed in all white darted from the cover of a white birch tree to the wider concealing hideout of an evergreen. It seemed his assailant was making their way around to the front.

It took only a second to shed his pants and boots and assume his wolf's shape. Stronger, faster, and definitely more deadly, Stu bounded out across the snow in a diagonal that left him open to the gunman but would hopefully draw attention away from Patricia and Ricky if they were in trouble.

Bang! The rumble of the missile fired didn't match the previous ones. Was Patricia returning fire? *Gotta love a woman with a gun.* So long as it wasn't aimed at him.

From behind the wide boughs of the evergreen, Stu's shooter stepped out. They raised their rifle. Not in Stu's direction, which could only mean … Pouring every ounce of adrenaline and strength he owned into the muscles of his legs, Stu bunched and leapt.

He wasn't in time to stop the gun from firing. Mid leap, he heard Patricia's gasp, and then he couldn't think, not when fury and fear took over. He hit the gunman, a figure slighter than expected, and together they landed in the snow, him atop, lips pulled back over his gums to display his teeth in a snarl.

In that moment, the wind blew past his nose, and the coppery scent of blood hit him. It didn't matter whose. A howl burst free from his throat, and he lunged, ready to kill. Gloved hands rose to block him. He snapped and strained, dodged the flailing fist, and would have darted in for a crushing bite—

"Stu! It's okay. I'm all right." Patricia's voice stayed him.

He swung his shaggy head and saw her jogging toward him in her slippers, her flannel pajamas a bright contrast to the snow. She appeared alarmed but unharmed. She dropped to her knees beside him. "It's okay, Stu. I'm not hurt. Ricky's been hit hard in the shoulder, a through and through shot, but he'll live too."

"And what of my brother?" a hostile, very much feminine voice demanded.

Both he and Patricia turned their gazes to the figure he still straddled.

His mate reached out a hand and removed the goggles to reveal a pair of very feminine eyes narrowed in hate, which, along with the taut lips, spoke of a person with some major anger issues. Of course, the whole gun/shooting thing might have aided in his psyche assessment. It wasn't hard to recognize the killer they'd caught once before. A killer who'd tracked them down to finish the job.

"You," Patricia snarled. "I was hoping I'd find you."

"You didn't try too hard. Good thing I was the one who came looking. And I asked you a question, animal. What happened to my brother?"

A cold grin the likes Stu hoped never to see turned his way graced Patricia's lips. "If you mean the other shooter dressed as your clone, then he's dead."

"Dead? You killed him?" The shriek almost made Stu wince.

"What did you expect?" Patricia spat, giving the female no quarter. "He shot my mate. Just like you were shooting at us too. I did what I had to in order to protect myself and Ricky."

"Filthy beast." The stupid female didn't seem to grasp the gravity of the situation. Insults weren't likely to help her argument or cause.

"Says the woman who has been travelling

from prison to prison murdering my kind."

"It's not murder to kill wild animals. But you will pay for killing my brother."

"I highly doubt that." Patricia sighed as she leaned back on her haunches. "I'm sorry for your loss, but despite your obvious hatred of our kind, I don't regret what I've done."

"Of course you don't. How can an animal understand what it's like to be human?" She sneered the reply, and Stu backed off her prone body, less some of her craziness infect him.

Patricia cocked her head and eyed the insane killer quizzically. "Why do you hate us? It's obvious you have some knowledge of what we are. But what could we have possibly done to make you hate us so much? Why the vendetta?"

"Because you're all beasts. Vile. Raping. Violent beasts. All I wanted was to do my job at the prison and get married. I was living a perfect life until the full moon when that monster came after me in the infirmary I was hired to clean. He snapped his cuffs like they were just paper and attacked me."

A shadow crossed Patricia's eyes. "I'm so sorry. That's not normal behavior for our kind."

"Normal?" The girl cackled. "How dare you use that word? You are all abominations that shouldn't exist. Because of that monster I lost everything. My job. My home. My mind." She emitted a high-pitched giggle. "It was my brother who devised the plan to get revenge. To cleanse the world of you *things*. How easy it was to spot you once I figured out what to look for."

"I don't know what you mean. Short of seeing

us shift, we are undetectable."

Her lips twisted into a nasty grin. "Are you? I had no problems. You're not as clever as you think. No one thinks to pay attention to a cleaning lady. The hardest part was getting hired by the different prisons. Once inside, I made it my mission to ferret you out."

"But you didn't do it alone."

"Why, when I had a brother more than willing to help? He knows his way around security. How simple for him to have cameras malfunction, or to get codes for me to slip in and get rid of you, one by one, starting with the bastard who hurt me. Such tragic accidents," she said with a mocking sneer. "And, to think, no one suspected."

"Wrong. We caught on."

"Not for a while." How proud the killer seemed of her accomplishment.

"I can understand going after the guy who raped you, but why kill the others? They never hurt you. Just like we never did anything to you. Why follow us out here?"

"Because you all must die."

So intent had they become on her words that they'd missed the subtle movement of her hands. But they couldn't ignore the forward slash of the knife that suddenly appeared in their attacker's grip. Stu had just a moment to knock Patricia sideways, the sharp slice of the blade cold against his skin then warm as blood streamed from the gash.

With a wild scream, the deranged human scrabbled to her feet and came after them, knife arcing for another slash.

Boom. The single shot threw her away, arms flailing, mouth open in a hissing scream that faded into silence. On his back in the snow, Stu only needed to tilt his head slightly to note their savior.

Ricky stood, bloodied, and none-too-steady on his feet, the gun in his hand dropping as if too heavy. "That was for Joey," Ricky mumbled before pitching face first into the snow.

Poor Patricia. Stu could see the horror in her eyes as she gazed from him to Ricky.

What a fucking nightmare this morning had turned out to be. Bodies they'd have to explain to the shifter council and also dispose of, lest human authorities question a little too deeply. Him in need of stitches before he bled out—the bitch wielded a sharp knife. Then add to the clusterfuck the fact that Ricky obviously needed a doctor before he bled out. Stu could only hope that Patricia wasn't too traumatized, else she'd probably run. Could things get any worse?

"Oh my god. My baby's been hurt."

Apparently, things could get a lot worse. Ma had arrived to the rescue, bundled in a bright blue parka atop snowshoes, and of course, she hadn't come alone. Stu almost welcomed the darkness brought on by blood loss so he wouldn't have to deal with the gaggle of brothers who swooped in to the rescue.

Chapter Twenty-Five

The cavalry arrived in time for the cleanup. As to how Stu's family knew to come, the killers had finally made a mistake. It seemed the human female's brother, some kind of tech guru, made some electronic inquiries that triggered an internal alarm with the shifter council. The shifter council turned around and notified the Grayson family. When they couldn't reach Stu on his cellphone—because his cell service didn't work in the mountains—they descended en masse to the rescue.

And chaos ensued.

Stunned by the fact not one but both of her lovers were grievously injured, Patricia went into a bit of shock. That lasted only as long as it took for Stu's mother to slap her out of it. Literally.

"Pull yourself together. These boys are too tough to die."

Patricia hoped so. As to the dead bodies and the crime scene?

It took a few days to sort the mess the dead humans caused. The bodies were disposed of in a deep ravine, where the wild animals would take care of them until some hapless hiker stumbled across them. Their hotel room was cleared out and all trace of them wiped as much as possible, not a difficult task given they were loners to begin with and their already criminal behavior kept them off the grid for the most part.

Patricia, though, only learned these details

later. At the time decisions were being made and evidence destroyed, she spent a harrowing ride speeding down the mountainside, one of Stu's brother's at the wheel. She sat in the back applying pressure on Ricky's wound while Stu's mother took care of her wolf. The local vet, an old grizzly shifter, was their closest medical ally, but as he joked, animals weren't that different from humans. Not the most reassuring of comments, or so he discovered when an ashen-faced Patricia pulled her gun and warned him that if he let them die, he'd follow.

But jokes aside, the guy was adept, and although Patricia spent some tense moments as he removed the silver bullet from Ricky, on the whole, the operation went smoothly.

Because of Ricky's shifter genes, he was soon on the path to recovery and chafing at the inactivity forced upon him. As for her wolf, Stu required a decent number of stiches to close his hero-induced wound, something his mother vented about, loudly and more colorfully than expected for a lady her size. But, with the danger from the killer a thing of the past and the guys on the mend, life in general returned to a more sane level.

Okay, maybe calling it sane was pushing it given Patricia brought home with her a wolf proudly displaying his thirty-four stiches and a panther who threatened to give him some more. But after the craziness she'd dealt with when Stu's family arrived to the rescue, a little too late but well meaning, the peace and quiet of her apartment was a soothing balm and, in the sudden quiet, suddenly too small.

She had nowhere to hide, especially once they

flanked her. Pinned by their dual gaze, she couldn't help a frisson of … fear or anticipation? She couldn't have said.

"Alone at last," Ricky said in a low purr.

"About freakn' time," Stu grumbled. "I thought my family would never leave us alone."

"They mean well," Patricia said, backing away from them even as her heart rate increased at the smoldering heat aimed her way.

"Mean well?" Stu snorted. "Ha. You'll learn. This is just the beginning. Now that you're part of my life, they'll be constantly over, harassing us."

Ricky laughed. "Poor puppy."

"Don't laugh, cat. I already heard Ma talking about how the poor orphan kitty needs some home-cooked meals to fatten him up."

That wiped the smile from Ricky's face. "I do not."

"According to her, you do. Oh, and she's already been talking to Aunt Jezebel about knitting you a wool sweater to keep you warm because she noticed you shivering in the cold."

"Because I was fucking naked in the snowy Rockies at the time. I don't need her taking care of me."

"Yeah, well good luck convincing my mother otherwise. She's mothered tougher men than you."

"I won't wear a yuppie sweater."

"You will," Stu told him in an ominous tone.

Patricia couldn't help but laugh. "You guys are too funny."

"Says the woman who will start receiving less-than-subtle hints about popping out a cub."

"A *baby*!" Patricia squeaked the word. "We're not even mated."

"Yet."

"Maybe not ever," she teased.

Ricky arched a brow. "Is it me, wolf, or did she just challenge us?"

"Oh, she definitely did," Stu agreed. "I think she wants us to convince her."

"Convince?" Ricky chuckled, a low sound that sent a shiver coursing through her. "I say we make her beg before we give her our mark and make her ours for a lifetime."

"What happened to waiting?" she asked, not at all perturbed by their talk of making her beg. One kiss, one touch, and she'd probably cave to their demands—and ask for more.

"Screw waiting. I'm taking what's mine."

"We both are," Stu added.

At their possessive claim, she just about came. Forget doubt, guilt, or anything else. She cared deeply for these two guys, wanted them and, after almost losing them, didn't want to spend another moment fighting what made her happy. Time to embrace the gift of a second chance fate had given her. Time to love again.

And she wanted to fuck, because dammit all, these past few days of taking it easy and having virtually no privacy had just about killed her, especially after experiencing the pleasure she could have at their two sets of hands—and cocks.

Afterward, she couldn't have said who moved first or how their clothes ended strewn on the floor, she did recall landing on her back on the bed, the mattress bouncing her only once before Stu swooped in to pin her as he nipped one of her nipples. The motion startled her into crying out, a cry that turned into a moan as his hot mouth sucked the erect tip of her breast. She couldn't figure out how the tug of his lips on her nipple somehow created a sensual link to her pussy. Who cared? She didn't want him to stop. To her delight, he cupped them and divided his attention between both breasts, and her pussy throbbed in approval.

But his wasn't the only mouth causing havoc. A groan slipped past her lips as warm breath puffed against her clit, teasing it, making her shiver in anticipation for what would come next. Lips brushed her already throbbing bundle of nerves. Ricky then rubbed the bristled edge of his jaw against it, the friction making her arch.

She gasped. "What are you doing?"

"Preparing you to beg."

Beg? Not quite, but she could demand. "Lick me."

He blew on her instead. "Those aren't the words I'm looking for."

"Eat me."

Ricky flicked his tongue across her clit, and her pelvis arched in reply. "Naughty cougar. You know what we want to hear."

"Although, it should be noted, at any other time, both those requests would be promptly obeyed," Stu chimed in.

She chuckled. She'd order her young wolf around with pleasure, later. Right now, she had a cat with a one-track mind to toy with. "Fuck me?" she asked hopefully.

Stu replied this time with a sharp bite to her nipple.

Her channel clenched, and her fingers scrabbled at the sheets as she squirmed under their dual erotic attack. Okay, perhaps she needed to stop teasing and give them what they all wanted. "Fine. Fine. You win."

"Say it," Ricky ordered.

"Please," Stu added.

"Take me." She paused for a moment, knowing the next words would forever change the course of her life for the better. "And mark me as your mate."

Two sets of mouths stilled. "I can't believe she said it," Stu said, his tone one of wonderment.

"Yeah, I thought for sure she'd wait until I got my dick out and beat her sweet pussy with it."

"Can't we still do that?" she asked.

"We can do anything you want, *bebé*. We have the rest of our lives."

"And, best of all, the rest of the night."

Stu caught her lips in a torrid kiss, and she sucked at his tongue, drawing it into her mouth and stroking it with her own. Somehow, she found herself straddling him, his cock tucked under her moist sex, trapped between their bodies, while Ricky slid in behind her, his muscled body pressed against her, the hardness of his shaft poking at her ass. His lips found the sensitive spot on the back of her neck, and he sucked it.

Oh my freakn' god. What decadence to be caught between two men, to have their naked bodies pressing against hers, skin to skin. Hot panting heat built and drove her wild with erotic hunger.

Something wet dribbled down the crack of her ass. Before Patricia could peek over her shoulder to see what Ricky was doing, Stu cupped her face and drew her forward for a kiss. Too busy with his tongue, she couldn't utter a word when a finger followed the liquid pooling in her crevice, a finger that rubbed moisture around her rosette. Her breathing quickened. Anal sex wasn't new to her. She'd experimented with Ryker. What she'd never done before was what she thought her guys had planned.

Was she ready for that kind of intimacy? Could she take both of them at once?

As if sensing her churning thoughts on the matter, Ricky distracted her. His fingers stroked her clit, his firm touch making her moan in Stu's mouth and turning her body boneless.

So aroused was she that the finger penetrating her ass slid in without hindrance. As a matter of fact, as Ricky continued to strum her clit, she rocked against the finger that stretched her tight hole. It was an odd sensation, not quite comfortable and, yet, not unpleasant at the same time. A second finger slipped into her rosette, easing the tightness of the ring. Good thing because, once those digits slid out, something much larger pressed against it. Knowing what to expect, she pushed out against the pressure of his cock easing its way in. He sheathed it and held still, a thick pulsing presence in her body that had her holding her breath.

She released it when he eased all the way back

out, leaving her empty and disappointed.

"Sit up," Ricky ordered.

Leaning herself to a position that raised her above Stu's body, she felt more than saw Stu's cock rise as if to follow her pussy.

She watched through half-slitted eyes as Stu gripped his shaft and guided it into her channel. Without being told, she slammed back down. Mmmm. That felt good.

And then things got really interesting.

"Lean forward."

She let herself fall forward, bracing herself on hands splayed across Stu's chest. Ricky's hands spread her cheeks, exposing her rosette for him. The thick head of his cock pushed its way back past the tight ring. And Patricia almost came.

It was almost too much. Filled and stretched and sandwiched between her lovers.

Every sensation, every breath, touch, slightest movement, everything became a sensual torture, an erotic delight, a decadence she savored.

But it was only just the beginning.

Ricky controlled the pace. With his hands on her waist, he slid her back and forth, a simple rhythmic motion that drew his dick in and out of her ass while, at same time, causing Stu's cock to thrust in and out of her sex.

Talk about mind-blowing. Caught in a never-ending orgasm, a wave of rapture that kept crashing over and over, she didn't think, didn't hesitate; she acted. In she swooped to capture the skin above Stu's heart with teeth that elongated without her even thinking of it. She pierced the skin with ease, leaving her mark on him. Stu arched, a deep thrust into her, and cried out, the liquid of his orgasm bathing her channel. Pushing herself back up and panting madly, she could barely say, "Bite me back."

He didn't need further encouragement. With a growl, Stu heaved forward and nipped her on the breast, a full, open-mouth bite that hurt … so good.

"My turn," Ricky announced. He'd no sooner spoken than she felt his teeth sink into her shoulder, and his cock, still buried to the hilt in her ass, jerked as he came. A dual mark to lay his claim.

Only one thing was left to be done. She turned her head, and he joined his lips to hers in a fervent kiss before breaking it off to bare his neck to her.

And, with one enthusiastic chomp, she sealed her fate, their fate. For good or ill, they were now joined.

Or, as Ricky put it in a smug, sated purr, "Now you belong to us, forever."

Which, if fate smiled upon them, would hopefully be a long, long time.

Epilogue

Sunday night dinner was more crowded and chaotic than ever, especially now that his brothers had someone new to pick on. Not that Ricky let them get away with it. The panther knew how to give as good as he got and fit in quite well with the Graysons.

Despite his statement that he'd not let Ma fuss over him, Ricky never did manage to use the word no around her. The bafflement on his face when she managed to get him to wear the hand-knitted wool sweater—blue and green with a big majestic moose on the chest—was priceless. Stu naturally got a picture and couldn't wait to hear his bellow of rage when he saw the posters he had done up with them for the youth center Ricky managed. The kids had helped in designing them, so like it or not, Ricky would have to smile and bear it. Oh, the fireworks it would create at home.

Home. Now there was a word he'd had to redefine. No longer did he live with his parents. Nope. After discussing it at length, they'd vetoed suburbia and upgraded Patricia's apartment and Ricky's bachelor pad to a townhouse downtown. Stu never thought he'd enjoy being a homeowner so much, but he couldn't deny the space was perfect with an office for him, a basement gym for Ricky, and a kickass shower in the master bath that was big enough for three, to Patricia's slick delight.

As to the relationship between him, Ricky,

and their cougar? While he and Ricky had their moments, they were short-lived and didn't result in too much damage. After Patricia finished tearing them a new one for fighting in the first place, all the heated emotions and adrenaline led to wicked makeup sex. Was it any wonder he sometimes purposely antagonized the cat? And he suspected Ricky of the same, especially when he went into his office and no sooner had he put his hand on his mouse than he was stuck to it. He got Ricky back a week later for the crazy-glue incident by greasing his barbells. And Patricia punished them both.

Good times.

It took less time than he'd expected to get Patricia to admit to the L word. It happened during one of her lectures to them about getting along or else she'd kill them. But Stu would treasure the declaration forever because, while it lacked the sappiness of a Hallmark card, it was heartfelt.

"God only knows why I love both of you idiots. But I do! Which is why I get so pissed when you fight," she'd shouted.

"You love us?" Stu repeated.

"Of course she does. How could she not? Well, me at any rate. I am, after all, awesome. And I have the bigger dick," Ricky retorted.

Before Stu could take offense, Patricia fired back. "I take that back. I love Stu. You, on the other hand, are a controlling, arrogant jerk." She'd thrown that challenge at Ricky with arms crossed under her heaving breasts. Was it any wonder Ricky got out the cuffs and used them on her so he could sensually torture—with Stu's help—until she admitted, at the top of her lungs, that she loved him too?

Another really good time.

God, he loved his new life and his freakn' cougar.

Feeling on top of the world, Stu grinned at the room at large, the new and improved dining room, which had to expand to accommodate the much-needed, larger table. They'd had to extend it, given Stu's new mated status.

Chris was in fine form this evening. A little bit drunk, and obviously not thinking with the right head, he tried to crack a few jokes about Stu enjoying the soap dropping so much in the slammer that he'd brought home his prison girlfriend. When Ricky clocked him in the jaw and laid him flat on the floor? Yeah, Stu high-fived the darned cat and told him he could have first turn at dessert later that night.

Patricia was less amused, probably because she was the dessert in question. But Stu would enjoy his punishment at her hands later. A shiver of anticipation went through him, and Patricia must have caught it because she squeezed his thigh and gave him a smile that warmed him through and through.

There was only one sobering thing to mar the Sunday gathering. The expanded table bore an empty seat with a place setting, a reminder and unspoken prayer for their brother, Derrick, whom they'd recently heard had gone missing in action during a routine scout of the desert while serving overseas.

Knowing his wily older sibling, Derrick was probably being held captive by a harem of women, and would emerge a hero who somehow singlehandedly won the war. Damned over achiever.

＊

When they finally rescued Derrick from the camp where the rebels held him captive, he was a shell of himself, a broken, dirty man who snarled at everyone, even those who would help him.

In order to survive, he'd relied on his beast a little too much. Returning to the man he once had been proved … difficult. Especially once it smelled *her*.

Lifting his eyes, which the mirror showed still glinted more wolf than man, Derrick leered at the chubby redhead in the ill-fitting blouse and slacks. Didn't they know better than to put someone so innocent, so delicate, so *human*, within reach? If they wouldn't do the right thing and lock him up, then he'd have to do the next best thing and scare her off before he did something he could never take back. *Like tear the clothes from her succulent body and dive between those creamy, curvy thighs.*

"Hello, darling," he drawled. "How nice of the military to send me a snack. I've been ever so hungry for a woman." He snapped his teeth at her and rumbled a low, menacing sound.

She didn't recoil though from his threat. Instead, she leaned forward and with a rolled-up folder smacked him on the nose. In a no-nonsense tone she said, "Bad wolf. Behave yourself right now, or there will be no treats for you!"

Say what?!

The End...only of this story. Freakn' Out is next.

CPSIA information can be o¹
at www.ICGtesting.com
Printed in the USA
LVHW02s050322⁰
587744¹